Rosie Hendry lives by the sea in Norfolk with her husband and two children. She is the author of the East End Angels series, an uplifting and heart-warming saga that follows the lives and loves of Winnie, Frankie and Bella, who all work for the London Auxiliary Ambulance Service (LAAS) during the Blitz. Listening to her father's tales of life during the Second World War sparked Rosie's interest in this period and she loves researching further, seeking out gems of real-life events which inspire her writing.

Keep up-to-date with Rosie by following her on Twitter, becoming her friend on Facebook or visiting her website:

@hendry_rosie
rosie.hendry.94
www.rosiehendry.com

Also by Rosie Hendry

The East End Angels series

The East End Angels

Secrets of the East End Angels

Christmas with the East End Angels

Victory for the East End Angels

The Mother's Day Club

The Mother's Day Victory

Rosie HENDRY

A Home from Home

SPHERE

First published in Great Britain in ebook in 2018 by Sphere
This edition published in 2022 by Sphere

1 3 5 7 9 10 8 6 4 2

All characters and events in this publication, other than those clearly in the public domain, are fictitious and any resemblance to real persons, living or dead, is purely coincidental.

A CIP catalogue record for this book is available from the British Library.

ISBN 978-1-4087-2656-3

Typeset in Bembo by M Rules
Printed and bound in Great Britain by Clays Ltd, Elcograf S.p.A.

Papers used by Sphere are from well-managed forests and other responsible sources.

Sphere
An imprint of
Little, Brown Book Group
Carmelite House
50 Victoria Embankment
London
EC4Y 0DZ

An Hachette UK Company
www.hachette.co.uk

www.littlebrown.co.uk

For my Mum, who lived at the real Catchetts Farm.

Norfolk, July 1944

Chapter One

Glorious sunshine, a skylark singing its crystal-clear notes overhead and the delicate scent of sun-ripened strawberries wafting towards her – Phylly Greenwood sighed happily as she pedalled the trade bike along the lane towards the village. This sort of day was perfect, so lovely that it deserved to be bottled up, preserved like summer fruits in a jam, ready to be brought out on days when being a Land Girl wasn't so lovely. Like the days in winter when the icy North wind roared across the fields and nipped at her nose and ears, while her fingers turned numb from picking frozen sprouts.

Phylly smiled to herself; she wouldn't change any of it, every job had its good and bad bits, and she knew that joining the Land Army was the best thing she'd ever done. If it wasn't for the fact that there was a war on, then life would be perfect.

Phylly glanced at her colourful cargo of strawberries nestling in their punnets in the basket at the front of her bike; picked before breakfast, they looked glossy, plump and delicious – she'd tasted a few as she'd picked and could vouch for how good they were. But dawdling along and daydreaming wasn't going to get her anywhere – the strawberries needed delivering to the village shop and she had a bus to meet. Gracie was coming back this morning and Phylly wanted to be there to meet her friend and fellow Land Girl. Knowing Gracie she was sure to come back to earth with a hard bump after her holiday, and if Phylly could be there to meet her it would help soften the blow. Hooking back a lose strand of her wavy blonde hair behind her ear, she pressed harder into her pedals and picked up speed.

*

'Phylly!' Gracie called out, smiling broadly as she ran down the steps of the bus, her brown leather suitcase clutched in one hand and the other hand checking that her neat red hat was still perched at a jaunty angle on top of her hair. 'What are you doing here?'

'Waiting for you.' Phylly threw her arms wide in welcome. 'I brought some strawberries to the shop, so I thought I'd wait and meet you off the bus and escort you back to the farm to make sure you come back.'

Gracie kissed Phylly's cheek and squeezed her friend's hands. 'Thanks for waiting for me, it's such a lovely surprise having you here.'

'You're welcome.' Phylly heaved the trade bike off its stand. 'Pop your case in the basket, it'll save you carrying it.'

Gracie did as she was told and slipped her arm through her friend's and they fell into step with Phylly pushing her bike.

'I don't suppose you've finished all the jobs and have nothing left for me to do?' Gracie asked as they walked through the village heading in the direction of

Catchetts Farm. 'I rather fancy having another day or two off relaxing in the sunshine.'

Phylly laughed. 'Never – if anything, there's even more. We were out picking the strawberries before breakfast this morning! Enough about work, tell me about your holiday – how's Richard?'

'Oh, he's wonderful.' Gracie let go of Phylly's arm and skipped on ahead a few paces, making her glossy dark brown curls bob around her shoulders. When she twirled back to face Phylly, her face was glowing with happiness. 'It was so lovely to be together again. It was bliss. We did lots of walking and talking, and just enjoying being together again.' She sighed. 'I only wish we had longer than a week.' A shadow clouded Gracie's face and her happiness suddenly dissolved, her large brown eyes sparkling with unshed tears. 'I didn't want it to end, Phylly. Saying goodbye this morning was so hard, I don't know . . .' her voice wobbled, 'when I'll see him again, or even if . . . He'll probably be flying on an op again tonight . . . '

Phylly pulled the bike onto its stand and put her arms

around Gracie, who'd fished a handkerchief out of her handbag and was dabbing her eyes with it. 'I know how much you worry about him, but try to focus on the wonderful time you've just had together and how much fun you had. I'm sure there will be plenty more good times for you in the future, too.'

'Will there? Are you sure?' Gracie looked up at Phylly, her face hopeful as if she was grabbing for a lifeline.

Phylly nodded. 'Now come on, everyone's looking forward to seeing you again and hearing about your holiday.'

Giving Gracie a final squeeze, Phylly wished that she could ease her friend's worries, but it was a bitter fact of wartime that nobody knew what the future held – whether a wife would ever see their husband return safely when it was all over, or not. Phylly glanced up at the sky, which was criss-crossed with white contrails against the clear blue, each one marking the path of men from the American air force out on their way to who knew where in their planes. How many of them would never come back again? Phylly understood Gracie's fears for her husband; just like those men up there, he risked his life every time he flew out over enemy territory. All they could do was hope he'd keep coming back, because Phylly knew the reality of losing someone in wartime and she desperately hoped it would never happen to her friend.

'Thank you.' Gracie stepped back and noticed Phylly looking upwards. 'Oh, look at that, all those men up there in broad daylight and anyone can see them for miles around, including the enemy.' She threw her arm up, pointing at the trails. 'They know they're coming and they'll be waiting for them.' Gracie shook her head. 'It's one small mercy that at least the RAF fly under cover of darkness, so Richard's not such a sitting duck as those poor men.' She shuddered. 'I suppose I should be used to it by now, but I'm not. I knew he was a flyboy when I married him, but it doesn't make it easier. I worry every night in case he's on an op.'

'I know,' Phylly spoke quietly, putting her hand on

Gracie's shoulder. She hated seeing her friend so worried and anxious when there was little she could do to help other than listen, reassure her and be there for her. Gracie was her best friend, the closest one she'd ever had, despite the vast difference in their backgrounds. Like chalk and cheese they were, Gracie with her plummy voice and well-to-do background and Phylly with her working-class upbringing. They'd probably never have come into contact, let alone become friends, if it hadn't been for the war, and she was glad that they'd been sent to work at Catchetts Farm together. Life in wartime wasn't all bad, despite the danger and worry being faced by people every day; some good things had come out of it, her and Gracie's friendship being one of them.

Phylly smiled at Gracie. 'Let's get you home and back into your Land Army uniform – there's work to be done, you know.'

Gracie nodded and managed a smile as she linked her arm through Phylly's. 'That's something I haven't missed, wearing our delightfully dull uniform,' she said, looking at the brown Land Army dungarees which Phylly was wearing. 'It's been so lovely to wear proper clothes.' Gracie smoothed down the skirt of her pre-war silk dress with its full swishing skirt and sighed. 'Come on, take me home if there's work to be done, at least working hard helps to take my mind off things for a while.'

London

'Can't I stay here with you? Please, Aunt Min, please don't send me away again.' Ten-year-old Jimmy Hopwood was trying hard to keep the threatening tears from flooding into his eyes. Inside, his stomach felt like it was clenching tighter and tighter, and his legs were lead-heavy, making it hard to walk in the direction of the place he so desperately didn't want to go.

Aunt Min stopped walking and turned to him, putting her hands on his shoulders so that they faced each other. As she looked down at him, Jimmy was sure her soft blue eyes were unusually bright behind her round glasses.

'We've talked about this before, Jimmy.' Aunt Min's voice sounded strange, as if it was being squeezed out of her. 'It's for your own safety cos London ain't safe any more with these flying bombs. I'm sorry, but there's no way round it but to evacuate you out to the countryside.'

'But we managed all right in the Blitz,' Jimmy reasoned. 'We survived that running down to the Underground when the bombers came.'

Aunt Min sighed. 'I know, but it ain't like that this time. Hitler's rockets don't come with much warning.' She rubbed his shoulders. 'I promised your father that I'd look after you, Jimmy, that I'd do the best I could for you and that's why you've got to go away. It's what he'd want you to do if he were still with us.'

'But what if it's like last time . . . ' Jimmy couldn't stop tears from spilling out.

Aunt Min fished a clean handkerchief out of her handbag and dabbed gently at his face. 'It won't be like last time, I promise you. You were unlucky, that's all, this time it'll be different. Come on now, we mustn't be late.' She put her arm around his shoulders and hugged her to him.

As they neared Liverpool Street station the pavements became crowded with mothers taking their children to be evacuated. Each child was carrying their belongings in a case or wrapped up in a brown paper parcel tied with string. Jimmy had his things in a small brown leather case which had belonged to his father. Every step he took nearer the station, felt like he was going to his doom. He'd done this before, had left home, gone to be safe and looked after in the countryside, only it hadn't turned out like it was supposed to. He felt shaky inside at the memory of what had happened. What if it happened again? Jimmy understood Aunt Min's reasons for why he should go, but if it was up to him he'd rather stay and face the risk that one of the flying rockets had his name on it than be evacuated again.

'Name.' The strange voice of the teacher interrupted

Jimmy's thoughts and he realised that while he'd been going over and over his worries in his head, they'd reached the station and it was nearly time.

'James Hopwood – Jimmy,' Aunt Min told the teacher.

The teacher ticked off his name and checked Jimmy's name tag which Aunt Min had carefully tied through a buttonhole on his coat. 'Right, quickly say your goodbyes and then Jimmy can join the line over there.' She turned briskly and started to deal with the next waiting child.

'Well, Jimmy, you look after yourself and remember your good manners. Write to me tomorrow to tell me where you are, and I promise I'll write straight back.' Aunt Min brushed at some invisible specks on his shoulders.

'Please . . .' Jimmy began in a last attempt to convince his Great Aunt.

'It *will* be fine this time, I know it will.'

Aunt Min bent down and kissed his check, her lavender smell so familiar and comforting that it made

Jimmy want to throw his arms around her and cling to her like a toddler. He could refuse to go, shout and scream and kick, but before he could do anything a strong arm was around his shoulder and leading him to the line, where the teacher left him, and by the time Jimmy looked back Aunt Min was gone.

He searched desperately for her in the sea of faces, but couldn't see her anywhere – there was no sign of her familiar face with her grey hair in its bun at the back of her neck and her old brown hat with the jaunty little feather sticking up perched on top of her head. She was all the family he had left now; he'd never known his mother as she'd died not long after he was born, and it was Aunt Min who'd brought him up. She was really his *Great* Aunt Min, his father's aunt and over seventy years old. She'd always looked after him when his father was away at sea on the merchant ships, a job he'd done before the war, and which had taken him to the bottom of the Atlantic after his ship had been hunted down by a U-boat. It was just him and Aunt Min left and now she had gone, and he was completely on his own.

A short while later Jimmy was seated in a train compartment with children he didn't know and the teacher who'd ticked him off the list. Outside on the platform the guard blew his whistle and the train started to glide smoothly out of the station. A few of the children were crying, but most seemed excited to be going. Jimmy stared out of the window, drinking in the last sights of London, the familiar-looking streets and buildings, the spaces where bombs had wiped out houses leaving gaps like missing teeth. As the train picked up speed, the buildings gradually thinned out and they sped out into open countryside. The sight of all the space and greenness made Jimmy's insides clench tighter. There was nothing he could do about it, nothing he could do to change what was happening to him. He felt completely helpless and alone, with no idea what his future held.

Catchetts Farm, Norfolk

Phylly and Gracie were met with the smell of freshly

cooked bread when they walked into the kitchen at Catchetts Farm.

'Oh, that smells lovely,' Gracie said, sniffing appreciatively.

Florrie Bray, her cheeks rosy from tending the oven, looked up from where she was turning loaves out of tins to cool. 'Gracie! Welcome back, my woman.' Dusting her hands down on her paisley-printed, cross-over pinafore, Florrie rushed over and gave Gracie a warm, welcoming hug, her petite frame a head height smaller than Gracie. 'Did you have a lovely time?'

'Yes, it was wonderful,' Gracie said, returning her embrace. 'Though the cooking at our guest house wasn't a patch on yours.'

Florrie laughed, making the corners of her blue eyes crinkle up, and she patted Gracie's arm. 'It's nice to be appreciated. It won't be long till dinnertime, rabbit stew and dumplings suit you?'

'Yes, please,' Gracie said. 'That's music to my ears.'

'I'll take your case upstairs for you,' Phylly said, 'then I'll get back to work.'

'The basket's ready for you to take out for the break when you come down, Phylly,' Florrie said, nodding at the full basket on the end of the table, making her thick grey curls bounce. 'They'll be gasping for a drink of cold tea.'

Phylly and Gracie's clattering footsteps up the wooden staircase brought Bea out of one of the bedrooms. 'Welcome back, Gracie!' Like her mother had downstairs, Bea put her arms around the Land Girl and gave her a warm hug. Bea was taller than her mother but looked similar with the same blue eyes and her thick hair, still a honey blonde which she wore in a victory roll at the nape of her neck. Stepping back, she studied Gracie's face. 'You certainly look like you've had a lovely time, plenty of rest and time with your husband – it's done you the power of good. I'm just finishing changing the bedrooms around, did Phylly tell you about the new sleeping arrangements?'

'No,' Gracie looked at Phylly. 'What's going on?'

'You're going to have to share your room with me

from now on, look . . . ' Phylly waved her arm, encouraging Gracie to peer in through the bedroom door. 'We've moved your room around to make space for my bed, it'll be like how you used to share a dorm at your old boarding school.'

Gracie shuddered. 'Don't remind me of boarding school. Cold rooms, awful food and terrible teachers – believe me, this can never be anything like that.' She frowned as she looked through the doorway at the room which had scarcely more than two feet between the two beds, just enough for a peg rug lying on the floor between them. 'Why's Phylly got to move in with me?'

'Because we're having an evacuee,' Bea explained. 'Your room's the biggest so it was a choice of putting the evacuee in with you or giving the evacuee Phylly's smaller room and having her move in with you. We thought you'd rather share with Phylly than an evacuee.'

'Quite right, too.' Gracie nodded. 'I'd definitely prefer to share with you than some strange child, Phylly, but I hope you don't snore.'

'Of course not,' Phylly said. 'Do you?'

'Absolutely not!' Gracie said, one hand on her hip. 'So, when's the evacuee arriving, Bea?'

'Today.' Bea's smile lit up her face. 'It'll be lovely to have a child about the place again. We had a couple of evacuees in thirty-nine, two young sisters. We loved having them here, but their mother missed them badly, so when nothing happened to London to begin with she came and took them home again.'

'What happened to them then, did they stay in London during the Blitz?' Phylly asked.

Bea shrugged. 'I don't know – the mother wrote to us for a little while, but then we didn't hear any more. I hope they survived.' She shrugged. 'Right, I'll get this done and come out and join you with the hoeing, Phylly. Gracie, once you've changed you'd better go and see Ned to find out what he wants you to do to start with.'

'No rest for me, then.' Gracie sighed dramatically. 'I was hoping for today off.'

Phylly laughed. 'No chance of that – you've had

your holiday, now it's back to work, so hurry up and change out of that fancy frock and get back into your dungarees because there's lots of fruit and veg to attend to.'

Gracie gave a mock salute. 'No wonder they call it the Land *Army*.'

'Just be grateful we don't have any square-bashing to do, like in the real army,' Phylly called over her shoulder as she went down the stairs. 'You wouldn't last five minutes.'

'No, I don't suppose I would,' Gracie called after her.

Bea laid a hand on her arm. 'It's good to have you back, Gracie. We've all missed you, especially Phylly.'

'I was lucky to be sent here with Phylly, she's a good friend. Keeps me on the straight and narrow.' Gracie's voice was serious, then she smiled at Bea. 'Time to swap my pretty dress for dungarees and an Aertex shirt and get on with doing my bit for the war effort.'

'That was good, Florrie.' Jacob Bray placed his knife and fork together on the empty plate in front of him and smiled warmly at his wife, his face crinkling up beneath his thatch of unruly white hair which never lay flat.

Florrie smiled across the table at her husband. 'You can't go wrong with rabbit stew and dumplings.'

Phylly looked at the older couple sitting near each other at the end of the scrubbed wooden table. They were a perfect pair, although complete opposites with Florrie being a small whirlwind of a woman who was never short of a thing to say, whereas Jacob was tall and quiet with an air of kind gentleness about him. They were both in their late sixties but still worked as hard as anyone else on the farm.

Catchetts Farm had become Phylly's home and she knew that she'd landed on her feet when she'd been sent to work here. Florrie and Jacob, and their son Ned and widowed daughter Bea, had all made her and Gracie so welcome that they were now like part of the family. Phylly thought how lucky they were; she'd heard awful tales from other Land Girls about how farmers treated them badly and cared nothing for their happiness. Catchetts Farm had become a real home to her, the first proper home she'd had since she'd shared one with her mother and brother. They'd been a close family, having pulled themselves together after her father had died when Phylly was just six. But that home, where she'd felt loved and wanted, didn't last . . .

'Nearly forgot, postman's been.' Florrie's voice brought Phylly's thoughts back to the present. 'I put them on the dresser.' Florrie got up from the table and took two letters from the dresser, passing one to Ned and the other to Phylly.

Phylly recognised the writing on the front of her letter at once – it was from her twin brother, John. He was somewhere in France with his Army engineering unit, rebuilding bridges or something like that, though Phylly knew this letter – like all the others – couldn't tell her exactly what he was doing because of the censor. She put the letter in her dungarees pocket to read later when she was on her own so that she could savour the contact with her brother, flimsy and distant as it was.

'We've got them!' Ned said from the other end of the table, waving his letter in the air. 'And they'll be starting tomorrow morning.'

'None too soon either,' Florrie said.

'Who's starting what?' Gracie asked.

'We've got two POWs, Italian ones, coming to work here,' Ned said.

'I didn't know we were having any POWs,' Gracie said.

'Nor did we for sure, until now.' Ned stood up and pushed his chair back under the table, signalling the end of the dinnertime break and the need to get back to work. 'Gracie and Phylly, can you start in the big greenhouse this afternoon? The tomato plants need checking over. Stake and tie up any that need it.'

Phylly nodded and started to collect the empty plates together, taking them over to the sink where Bea was pouring hot water from the kettle into the sink for the washing up.

'Bea, what time are we going to meet the evacuee?' Phylly asked.

'They're supposed to be there at five o'clock. I expect the poor little thing will be worn out after all that travelling.'

'Can I come with you?'

Bea looked at Phylly, her blue eyes wide in surprise. 'Well, yes, if you want to.'

'I'd like to, it would be nice to welcome them here.'

'Why do you want to go and get the evacuee?' Gracie asked, as she and Phylly went outside and headed across the farmyard towards the big greenhouse. 'You'll see them soon enough when they get here.'

'Because I know what it's like to be sent to live with strangers,' Phylly told her. 'I remember know how it feels, and if I can go along and help our evacuee feel a bit happier then that's what I'd like to do.'

'But you weren't an evacuee, were you?'

'No.' Phylly paused while she opened the greenhouse door and they stepped through it into the warm, humid heat, which was infused with the sharp tang of tomato plants. 'But my brother and I were sent to live with a stranger after our mother died.'

'What about your father, couldn't he look after you?'

'No, he died before she did, when I was six. He'd never truly recovered from being gassed in the Great War and pneumonia finally carried him off one winter.'

'I'm sorry, I didn't know,' Gracie said.

Phylly shrugged and smiled at her friend. 'There's no reason you should have, we've never talked about it.'

'Was your aunt nice, were you happy living with her?'

Phylly's stomach twisted at the memory of that time, of how shocking it had been to go from the warm, loving home with their mother, to live with a woman who didn't really want them. She'd done her duty and taken them in, fed and clothed them, and for that she was grateful, but her aunt didn't have a maternal bone in her body. There'd been no warmth, no understanding or love for her and her brother. They'd had to rely on each other and grow up quickly.

'She was . . . adequate . . . gave us a place to live but it was hard because we'd never met her before. She felt like a stranger and she lived in a strange place. We went from living in a small village where everyone knew each other to living in a city, far away from the green space we'd been used to. It would have been much worse if John and I hadn't had each other to rely on.' Phylly sighed. 'It was a harsh contrast from the loving home we had before, but it could have been a lot worse. I just want to make sure the evacuee feels welcome and help them settle in. You know, you could come tonight too, if you want.'

Gracie shook her head. 'I might scare them. I'm not very good with children, being an only child.'

'You'll soon get used to them. Bea's going to enjoy having a child to fuss over, she'll be like a mother hen. If she hadn't been widowed so young, she'd probably have had a whole brood of children to love by now.' Phylly picked up a ball of twine and a penknife from the bench inside the door. 'Things are changing here at Catchetts, with an evacuee coming and then two POWs.'

'Humph!' Gracie pulled a face. 'I don't like the sound of them – why do we need them here?'

'To help us get all the work done.'

'Don't we work hard enough?' Gracie asked, one hand on her hip.

'Of course we do, but there's such a lot to do, especially at this time of year, and two extra pairs of hands will make a big difference.'

Gracie sniffed. 'They'll probably be a couple of shirkers.'

'Or they might be good workers. I'm looking forward to meeting some Italians, maybe learning some Italian. I thought you'd be pleased – you've told me how much you loved travelling abroad before the war, and didn't you especially like Italy for all the good-looking chaps there?'

Gracie glared at Phylly for a moment. 'That was different,' she snapped. Without saying another word, she stalked off to the far end of the greenhouse and started work.

Phylly stared at her friend, wondering what on earth had got into her.

*

'We're nearly there, everyone,' the teacher called out from the front of the bus.

They'd swapped the train for a bus at a small country station, and it was now taking them the final few miles to their destination. The teacher had explained that they were now in the county of Norfolk, but wherever that was Jimmy had no idea – he'd never heard of it before, so it might have been near the moon for all he knew. But wherever it was, it felt a very long, long way from home and Aunt Min.

Jimmy's heart was thumping hard when the bus finally came to a stop outside a small hall. Somehow his legs managed to carry him off the bus and he followed the other children into the hall where ladies in the green uniform of the WVS stood waiting for them.

'Line up, everyone.' A cheerful WVS lady herded them into an orderly queue. 'There are sandwiches and cocoa for you all before you go off to your new homes.'

Jimmy was hungry, but when it came to his turn to take a plate of fish-paste sandwiches, he couldn't. He didn't want to eat because his stomach was knotting up again, and he'd already been sick once on the train, when his worrying had got too much.

'No, thank you,' he said, remembering his good manners.

He saw the WVS lady staring at the stains on his clothes – the teacher had done her best to clean him up, but there was no doubt that he didn't look or smell as clean as he had when he'd left home that morning. Aunt Min had made sure he was bathed and wearing his best clean clothes, including the pullover she'd knitted him.

The WVS lady nodded sympathetically at him. 'Don't worry, you'll eat when you're ready, we don't want to upset your stomach any more.'

Jimmy smiled at her gratefully and went to sit alongside the other children who were ravenously eating their food. He knew that once they'd finished it wouldn't be long before the choosing would start. Already there were strange grown-ups gathering just inside the doorway looking at them all and working out which of them they wanted. Jimmy remembered how it went, how they'd sit waiting for someone to offer them a home, how it made him feel like something in a market waiting to be sold. The nice-looking, neat and tidy girls would go first, and the boys who looked strong and able to work well on a farm. The children left over would be the second pickings, the ones who'd been passed over before. Jimmy knew with the state he was in he wasn't going to be anyone's first choice, and he stared down at the floor, wishing over and over that he was back home with Aunt Min.

They were late.

Today of all days, some of the chickens had made a break for freedom and found a way out of the orchard into the next field and had been happily scrapping up young cabbage plants. Everyone had had to help round them up and put them back where they belonged before they caused too much damage.

Now five o'clock had come and gone and Phylly and Bea were pedalling fast towards the village to meet their evacuee. By the time they reached the village hall they'd passed several evacuees already on their way to their new homes with people from the village.

'Do you think there'll be any children left?' Phylly asked as they propped their bikes against the outside of the village hall.

'I hope so.' Bea straightened her hat, which had slipped in their haste to get there.

Walking into the hall, Phylly's eyes were immediately drawn to the few children left, who were sitting on the row of chairs in the middle of the room. There was a group of four children clinging on tightly to each other, brothers and sisters going by how similar they looked, and who were clearly desperate not to be parted, and one other boy who was sitting on his own staring down at the floor. Phylly and Bea looked at each other and didn't need to say a word – he was the one for them.

'Oh, thank goodness you're here, Mrs Fenton.' A WVS lady came rushing over to them, looking very flustered. 'I'd begun to think you'd changed your mind about giving an evacuee a home.'

Bea smiled at her. 'Of course not, Mrs Taylor. We had an emergency with some escaped chickens just as we were about to leave, and they had to be rounded up before they caused any more damage.' Bea paused and nodded towards the boy sitting on his own. 'We'd like to give a home to that young lad there, if he's willing.'

'Very well, though I should warn you, he was poorly on the way here,' the WVS woman explained in a hushed tone. 'His clothes are in a bit of mess, I'm afraid.' She paused, as if she expected Bea to change her mind.

'Poor little fellow,' Bea said, not in the least put off. 'Then we'd best get him home quick and into something clean, hadn't we? Phylly will you go and ask him to come with us while we sort out the paperwork?'

Phylly's heart was skipping inside her chest as she walked over to the boy who looked so forlorn and alone. Memories of her and her brother's arrival at their aunt's flashed through her mind, but she quickly stamped them down. It wasn't going to be like that for this boy, she'd make sure of that.

'Hello.' She squatted down on the floor so that her eyes were level with his. 'My name's Phylly, what's yours?'

The boy looked startled, and then replied, his voice barely a whisper. 'Jimmy Hopwood, miss.'

'Well, Jimmy, would you like to come and live with me and Bea – that's her in the green dress.' As he looked over to where Bea was talking to Mrs Taylor, Phylly noticed how tired he looked, his dark blue eyes were smudged underneath, and his hands were so tightly clenched together that his knuckles stood out white. 'We live at Catchetts Farm outside the village, it's a lovely place. I've lived there for nearly four years, so I can vouch for it being a good place to live.'

Jimmy looked down at the floor for a few moments, saying nothing, and it seemed to Phylly as if he was trying to work out something, then he met her eyes and nodded.

'Let me take your case for you.' Phylly picked up Jimmy's case and held out her other hand for him to take. He hesitated for a moment and then slipped his hand in hers. Phylly gave it a reassuring squeeze and led him over to Bea. 'This is Jimmy Hopwood, Bea.'

'Hello, Jimmy,' Bea smiled at him warmly. 'I'm very pleased that you're going to come and live with us, and I hope you'll be happy.'

'Hello,' Jimmy spoke quietly.

'Phylly, Mrs Taylor's short of help tonight so I'm going to stay and help with the clearing up, so can you take Jimmy home for me?' Bea asked.

'Of course,' Phylly smiled. 'We'll see you back at the farm.'

For the second time that day, Phylly walked out of the village pushing her bike with a suitcase stowed inside the basket at the front, only this time her companion was nothing like the talkative Gracie. Jimmy hadn't said a word since they'd left the village hall, so Phylly was doing her best to get a conversation going.

'There's the school,' Phylly nodded at the old Victorian building as they went past. 'I expect you'll start there once they've sorted out a timetable. I think the last time evacuees came there were so many children that they had to go in shifts, some in the morning and some in the afternoon. Do you like school?'

Jimmy didn't say anything, just shook his head.

'I didn't either. Too much sitting still for me, though I liked learning new things – still do. I've learned so much since I joined the Land Army, real-life useful stuff about growing food, things like strawberries, we've got lots ripening now. Do you like strawberries?'

Jimmy nodded.

'You'll be able to have some tomorrow, then,' Phylly smiled at the boy, her heart squeezing at the thought of how he must be feeling. 'Have you ever picked your own strawberries be—' Phylly stopped talking. A plane was flying low above the fields, its engines roaring, making the air throb with the noise. 'That Spitfire's almost hedgehopping his way along.' Laughing, Phylly waved her arm above her head.

'Don't!' Jimmy shouted, grabbing at her arm and pulling it down. 'It's a German!'

A German plane! Phylly was stunned. What had she

done? How could she have been so foolish? Had the pilot seen them? Her question was soon answered as the plane banked steeply over the village and turned back towards them. Phylly stared at it, transfixed and unable to move, as it flew towards them, coming in fast and low.

She'd heard about German planes strafing the ground with bullets, easily picking off people out in the streets, and here she and Jimmy were, out in the open with nowhere to hide, just sitting ducks in the middle of the road. All she could think about as the plane bore down on them was: had Jimmy's family sent him away to keep him safe, only to have him meet his end here?

Chapter Two

Something was stinging Phylly's arm and she could smell the earthy scent of damp soil close to her face. Lifting her head, she saw that one of her bare arms was lying on crushed nettles. She quickly pulled it out of the way and then she remembered . . . the German plane . . . it had been coming in fast . . . Phylly shuddered. She could still hear its engines, but their roaring and throbbing was getting fainter. And Jimmy . . . where was he?

A wave of panic surged through Phylly. Struggling to ease herself up from where she lay sprawled on her front, she became aware of a weight pressing down on her legs. Looking back over her shoulder she saw it was Jimmy, lying further down the ditch, partly covering her legs. He looked at her and smiled. He was alive! Phylly closed her eyes and sent up a silent prayer.

'You all right?' Jimmy asked, starting to sit up.

Phylly reached out to try and stop him. 'Keep down! The plane.'

'It's gone.' Jimmy said. 'Listen.'

She listened hard, trying to pick up any sound of engines, but all she could hear were the peaceful sounds of the countryside, a skylark singing its heart out somewhere overhead and the happy chatter of swallows diving for insects in the early evening air.

'You've got to hide when German planes are around,' Jimmy said, standing up. Phylly was relieved to see that he was unharmed apart from a generous smudging of soil and some bleeding scratches on his bare knees.

She slowly raised herself up to a sitting position, not

daring to stand straight up like Jimmy because she felt shaky and her heart was still pounding. 'How'd we get in here?'

'I pushed you in. Hope you don't mind.' Jimmy grinned at her. 'Only we could've been shot standing in the middle of the road.'

Phylly nodded, remembering those awful few seconds which had seemed to slow down as the plane bore down on them. She hadn't known what to do. She'd just stood there, watching and waiting. If it hadn't been for Jimmy . . . She vaguely remembered him grabbing hold of her arm, pushing her to the side of the road and down into the safety of the ditch.

'I'm sorry, I didn't know what to do,' Phylly said. 'Thank you for saving us.'

Jimmy shrugged. 'We're used to German planes coming after us in London. You just have to get out of the way.'

Phylly nodded at the boy who had experienced far too much danger already in his young life. It was a shocking sign of what war did, when children like Jimmy knew how to protect themselves from enemy planes.

'Did he shoot? I didn't hear anything.'

'No, I watched him. He just dipped his wings at us, like he was saying hello. We were lucky.'

'Thank goodness,' Phylly sighed. From where she was sitting in the ditch, she could see her bike lying abandoned on its side in the middle of the road, with Jimmy's brown leather case spilling out of the wicker basket.

'You've been stung.' Jimmy pointed to her arm, which was covered in reddened lumps where she'd landed on the nettles.

'It's nothing to worry about.' Phylly looked around at the bottom of the hedge behind the ditch and saw what she needed - a dock plant. She plucked a leaf, crushed it in her hands and rubbed it over her throbbing stings. 'This'll help. Your scratches need cleaning up properly, though. Come on, we need to get you home.'

Phylly stood up slowly, taking some deep breaths to steady herself. Everything was fine, she reassured herself – they'd been lucky, and all she needed to do now was get Jimmy safely home. But before she could climb out of the ditch, she heard the sound of another engine coming towards them, only this time along the road.

'Something's coming! I'll move your bike.' Jimmy scrambled out of the ditch and dashed towards the bike in the middle of the road.

'Jimmy!' Phylly shouted after him. She watched in horror as a jeep came around the corner, going far too fast and heading straight towards where Jimmy was struggling to pick up the heavy bike. Again, time seemed to slow – Phylly watched helplessly as the driver braked hard and skidded to a halt just a few yards from Jimmy.

Phylly's stomach twisted in shock and she closed her eyes. Twice in a matter of minutes, the boy whom Bea had entrusted her to escort safely home had nearly been hurt. When she'd decided to come and meet the evacuee and welcome them to their new home, this wasn't what she'd planned.

'Are you OK? Did you fall off?' an American voice said. Phylly opened her eyes and saw that an American serviceman, the driver of the jeep, was helping Jimmy to pick up her bike.

'I'm all right,' Jimmy told him. 'We dropped the bike to hide from the German plane. Did you see it?'

'I sure did. He's a crazy pilot flying about here with your Spitfire boys around.'

A sudden rush of anger raced through Phylly. 'You were going too fast!' she shouted at the American. 'You nearly ran him over.'

He turned to look at her and removed his peak cap from his dark blonde hair. 'I'm sorry, miss. I didn't mean to . . . ' he paused, running his hand through his hair, 'but you're right, I *was* going too fast, it was the excitement of finally finding—'

'But I'm all right,' Jimmy interrupted. 'No harm done, honestly.'

The American walked over to the ditch and held out his hand to Phylly. 'Can I help you out?'

'Thank you.' Phylly took his hand and climbed out

of the steep-sided ditch. 'When you're driving around here, you've *always* got to expect that *anything* might be round the next corner: a horse and cart, cows on their way to milking or . . .'

'A child. I'm sorry, truly I am, miss, and in future, I promise to remember what you said. Are you OK, are you hurt?'

Phylly shook her head. 'Just a few nettle stings and a bit shaken up that's all, but Jimmy's legs are scratched so I need to get him home to clean them up.'

'You look kinda pale and in shock, if you don't mind me saying so.' The American's voice was kind. 'I'd like to take you both to be checked out at the base on the other side of the village. It's not my base, but I'm sure they'll help out.'

'No, thank you, we'll be fine,' Phylly said, trying hard to sound normal.

'I'm Edwin Johnson.' He held out his hand to Phylly.

'Phylly Harper.' Shaking his hand, she noticed what extraordinarily blue eyes he had, like the clearest blue of a summer sea. 'And this is Jimmy Hopwood, just evacuated from London today.'

'Pleased to meet you both.' Edwin shook Jimmy's hand. 'I really do think you should be checked out – what do you say, Jimmy? I could take you there in the jeep and then back home afterward.'

'What about Phylly's bike?' Jimmy asked.

'That's no problem, we'll put it in the back of the jeep.'

Jimmy looked at Phylly for an answer. Should she accept Edwin's kind offer of help or just walk home on legs which felt as if they were filled with jelly and liable to wobble over at any moment? The sensible thing was to accept.

'Very well then, thank you.'

Jimmy sat in the back of the jeep; the wind blowing his hair back felt welcomingly cool, and the sweetness in his mouth was delicious, a rare treat with sweets being in such short supply with the rationing. His mind was full of the things he'd just seen. He'd never dreamed he'd ever go on an American airbase and meet lots of Americans with their strange voices, like in the Saturday morning films at the pictures. His scratches had been cleaned and bandaged up, he'd been given sweets – or what they called candy – to eat, seen the huge bombers and was now was being driven home in a jeep.

'Home' wasn't the right word for it, because his home was in London with Aunt Min, but he was on his way to the place Phylly, the nice Land Girl, called Catchetts Farm. The place he was being evacuated to and had started to go to before the German plane came along.

He should have been there by now. He was late. Very late. Jimmy's stomach knotted – what would they say? What would they do? He remembered what had happened before when he'd been late home. Jimmy wished he could stay riding in the jeep for ever and never reach the farm. Aunt Min had said it would be different this time, but how could she know for certain?

It seemed like only a few short minutes before Phylly

turned around from her seat in the front of the jeep, where she'd been showing Edwin the way, and said, 'That's Catchetts Farm,' as they turned off the road and onto a lane that led to a farm.

When they came to a halt in the farmyard in front of a red brick farmhouse, the sweetness in Jimmy's mouth had gone, leaving a parched dryness. Before they could get out of the jeep, the door of the farmhouse opened and the woman he'd met at the village hall earlier, Bea, came rushing out, followed by four other people. Jimmy shrank back in his seat. Did she look angry?

'Phylly! Jimmy!' Bea said breathlessly. 'Are you all right?' Her eyes scanned them both, settling on Jimmy's bandaged knees. 'What happened?'

'We're fine, honestly,' Phylly said, climbing out of the jeep.

'What's wrong with Jimmy's legs?' Bea asked.

After Phylly had explained what had happened and how Edwin had come along and helped them, Bea held out her hand to him. 'Thank you for helping them, I appreciate it.'

Edwin smiled and shook her hand. 'I'm glad I could help, ma'am.'

'Phylly, will you bring Mr Johnson in for a cup of tea while I sort Jimmy out?' Bea lifted his case out of the jeep. 'Jimmy, you come with me and we'll get you changed into some clean clothes.' She held out her hand to him.

Jimmy hesitated. He knew what was coming.

'It won't take long, Jimmy,' Bea reassured him. 'Then you can meet everyone properly and have something to eat.'

It wasn't that which was holding him back. It was something much, much worse. Jimmy knew he had to go, so he took hold of Bea's hand as he climbed down out of the jeep, and she kept hold of it as she led him into the farmhouse. He hardly noticed the inside, and although a delicious smell of cooking did filter through a crack in his fear, Jimmy pushed that aside. He had to concentrate on what was going to happen and prepare himself.

'This is your room,' Bea said when they reached the

landing. She opened the door, led him inside and put his suitcase on the bed.

As soon as she let go of his hand to open his case, Jimmy dashed across the room and stood against the far wall, pressing his back against it, wishing it would open up like in a magical story so he could hide inside. His heart was racing, and he felt like an animal cornered by a huge predator.

'If you change out of your clothes and put some clean ones on, I can take the dirty ones down to wash . . .' Bea stopped talking and stared at him. 'Jimmy? Whatever's the matter?'

She stepped towards him. Jimmy felt his body tense and he couldn't stop himself from flinching.

Bea gasped and stepped back. 'I'm not going to hurt you.'

Jimmy started to shake – his throat hurt and tears smarted in his eyes.

'Has someone hurt you before?' Bea spoke gently.

Jimmy nodded.

'At home?'

He shook his head. Aunt Min would never hurt him.

'Where?'

'Last time,' Jimmy croaked. 'Last evacuation.'

Bea knelt down in front of him so that their eyes were level and Jimmy saw that her blue eyes were shiny with tears. She laid her hand gently on his shoulder. 'I promise you, Jimmy, with all my heart, that no one will hurt you here. We're all pleased to have you come and stay with us.'

Jimmy couldn't stop the tears from running down his face as his body shook with relief. This was so different from before. When he'd been evacuated just before the start of the war, the old couple he'd been billeted with hadn't wanted an evacuee. They'd been forced to take him because they'd had room in their house, but he'd been as unwelcome to them as any mouse in a pantry. He couldn't ever do anything right for them, no matter how hard he'd tried, and was always being punished for the least little thing.

'You're not . . . angry . . . about me . . . being late?'

'Angry?' Bea frowned. 'Of course not. I was worried

when I got back and you weren't here, but I'm not angry, not one little bit, just glad you're here and safe.' She paused. 'Was someone angry with you for being late before?'

Jimmy nodded. 'They beat me when I was late home from school . . . only five minutes.' The one time he'd been late, the old man had taken his belt to him and given him a hiding to remember it by. Jimmy thought it was strange that they should have been so angry about him being five minutes late when they didn't even want him there in the first place.

Bea bit her bottom lip. 'How long were you there?'

'Six weeks. I wrote to Aunt Min begging her to come and take me home, but they burnt all my letters so she never got them.' Jimmy swallowed hard at the memory of that miserable time. 'But she was worried and came to find me . . . she took me home again.'

Bea gently took hold of his hands in hers. 'We'll write to your Aunt Min tonight and tell her where you are and invite her to come and visit as soon as she likes, then she'll be able to see for herself that you're safe and wanted here. Would you like that?'

Jimmy nodded, feeling like a heavy weight had slipped off his shoulders. Aunt Min had been right when she'd promised it would be fine this time.

Bea smiled at him. 'Now get yourself changed out of those clothes and into some clean ones. I'll wait outside the door for you, and then we'll go downstairs and get you something to eat.'

Jimmy smiled at her. He suddenly felt very hungry.

'Are you sure you won't have something to eat?' Florrie asked Edwin as he stood up ready to leave. 'There's plenty to go around.'

'No, thank you, ma'am. I gotta get back to the base before my pass runs out. A cup of tea was just fine.' Edwin picked up his cap from the kitchen table.

'Then come to tea on Sunday afternoon,' Bea said, ladling soup into a bowl for Jimmy, who was now sitting at the table. 'We'd like to thank you properly for helping Phylly and Jimmy. Say three o'clock, if you'd like to come.'

'I sure would, thank you, ma'am.' Edwin smiled making his striking blue eyes crinkle up at the corners. 'I'll look forward to it.'

Phylly followed Edwin outside. 'I really appreciate your help tonight, and I'm sorry that I shouted at you the way I did. I shouldn't have, it was just . . . '

'Apology accepted, but I deserved it because I was going too fast. Don't worry, I'll remember what you said about what might be waiting for me around corners.' He smiled and held out his hand. 'I'm glad I met you today, Phylly. Is that short for something?'

'Phyllis,' she said, shaking his hand.

'I'll see you Sunday afternoon, Phylly.' Edwin climbed into the jeep and started the engine. 'Don't go jumping in any more ditches, now.' He smiled, touched the peak of his cap and drove away.

With another of Florrie's filling breakfasts inside them, Phylly and Gracie sat on the low wall outside the farmhouse door, tying up the laces of their sturdy brown leather shoes.

'Hope we're not working in the greenhouses today,' Gracie said. 'It was baking in there yesterday.'

'Could be more strawberry picking, or there's the . . . ' Phylly stopped as Ned appeared out of the tool shed and strode towards them carrying hoes. 'There's your answer, Gracie.'

'Can you start with tidying up the cabbage plants in Two Acres?' Ned handed them both a hoe as they stood up. 'Best to knock back the weeds before they get a chance to . . . ' He paused at the sound of an engine rumbling down the lane towards the farmyard.

'An army truck, what's that doing here? Has there been an invasion or something?' Gracie shielded her eyes against the sun, watching as the large, canvas-covered truck drove into the yard and came to a halt with a jerk of brakes.

'That'll be our POWs,' Ned said.

Phylly glanced at Gracie, who'd had the strangest reaction to hearing about the POWs yesterday. How was she going to react now they were finally here? To Phylly's surprise, her friend remained silent, but her face had turned pale and wore an odd stony expression.

'Catchetts Farm? Mr Bray?' a soldier asked out of the open window.

'That's right.' Ned said. 'We're expecting two POWs.'

'Good cos that's what we've brought you.' The soldier jumped out of the cab and banged hard on the wooden sideboards of the truck as he walked around to the back. 'Let's be 'aving yar,' he bellowed, pulling down the tailgate.

Two POWs dressed in identical chocolate-brown uniforms jumped down. 'Right on the double, quick march,' the soldier barked at their heels like an angry terrier.

The men marched towards where Phylly and the others stood waiting. They'd been joined by Jacob, Florrie and Bea, who'd heard the truck arrive and come outside.

'Halt!'

The POWs stopped and stood to attention, staring straight ahead.

'All yours then. We'll be back to get them at five o'clock. If they give you any trouble, you let me know.' The soldier narrowed his eyes, his thin weaselly face looking as if he hoped there would be.

Phylly thought he looked like the sort who would enjoy dealing with trouble and she hoped for the prisoners' sake that everything would be fine, no problems and nothing for the soldier to bother about.

'I'm sure there—' Ned began.

'Five o'clock then,' the solider interrupted, climbing into the truck's cab where the driver started the engine and with a crunching of gears, they drove out of the yard.

The moment the truck left, Phylly sensed the two prisoners relax. They stood still, looking ahead, but they no longer looked as if they were stretched taut, on full alert.

'Welcome to Catchetts Farm. I'm Ned.' Ned held out his hand to the older POW. 'We're pleased to have you come and work here.'

Both men looked surprised at his greeting, but immediately responded with a warm smile and each shook Ned's hand enthusiastically.

'*Buongiorno*, hello. Thank you for welcome,' the older man said, bobbing his head. 'I am Benedict and this Roberto, he no speak English, I help him.'

Ned introduced the men to everyone else, explaining who was who, and everyone in turn received a warm response from the two Italians, shaking hands and making them feel welcome.

When it came to Gracie's turn, she merely said 'Hello,' her voice sounding cold and stiff as if it was being forced out of her. Ignoring Benedict's outstretched hand, she announced, 'I'll go and get on,' and without waiting for a response, turned and strode off towards Two Acres.

'Gracie?' Phylly called after her, but she didn't look back. What on earth had got into her? Ignoring Benedict's hand was rude, and the way she'd said hello was so grudgingly spoken she might as well not have bothered.

Phylly caught Florrie's eye – she was obviously shocked at Gracie's behaviour too.

'Have you done farm work before?' Ned asked.

'*Si*, for two year,' Benedict replied. 'We plant potatoes, stack corn, hoe fields . . . ' He shrugged and smiled, his blue eyes standing out against his tanned face. 'Lot work but is good to be busy.'

Ned smiled. 'This is a market garden farm, we don't grow corn here, just fruit and vegetables, but there's plenty of hoeing to do. You can start on the cabbage plants this morning with Phylly, here. She'll help you out if you need anything.'

'Thank you,' Benedict said, before turning to Roberto and speaking to him in rapid, lilting Italian.

Although Phylly couldn't understand a word of what he said, she liked the sound of it and hoped that perhaps they might teach her some Italian sometime.

'That wasn't very welcoming, Gracie,' Phylly said as she reached the far side of the field where her friend was hoeing between the small cabbage plants. She'd settled the Italians into their work and made straight for Gracie to try to find out what was going on. 'You were very rude to them and that's not like you.'

Gracie stopped work and glared at Phylly. 'I wasn't *that* rude. I said hello, didn't I?'

Phylly shook her head, sighing. 'Yes, but with all the warmth and welcome of a spitting cat! Working on the far side of the field from them isn't very friendly either. Ned wants us to keep an eye on them and help them out if they have a problem.'

Gracie tucked a stray curl back into her headscarf, which was tied turban-style around her hair. 'You can do that, can't you?'

'Yes, of course—'

'Then where's the problem? If they need help, *you* can help them, it doesn't take both of us. Now if you'll excuse me, I have work to do . . . ' Gracie chopped down a weed with more force than necessary, narrowly missing taking down some cabbage plants with it.

Phylly reached out and touched Gracie's arm. 'What's the matter? I don't understand your attitude to the POWs – ever since you knew they were coming you've been strange about them. They seem really nice people,' she paused, listening, and smiled. 'Can you hear that? They're singing.'

'Humph!' Gracie snorted. 'I told you they'd be shirkers.'

Phylly sighed. 'If you bothered to look, you'll see that they're singing *while* they work. Look!' Both men were working, moving steadily along the rows, the yellow circles on the back of their brown uniforms making them stand out clearly in the field.

Gracie deliberately turned her back so that she couldn't see them and carried on viciously chopping at weeds.

Phylly stared at her friend, who was normally so polite and well mannered. There was something odd going on here, but Gracie obviously didn't want to talk about it and the atmosphere around her was extremely chilly.

'I think I'll go and work closer to Benedict and Roberto, it'll be easier to help them out if they need it.'

Phylly left Gracie to stew in her strange mood and walked back across the field. She liked the idea of listening to singing as she worked; both men had fine voices, and though she didn't understand a word of it, it certainly sounded lovely. If Gracie chose to shut herself away from it, then that was her choice. Whatever it was that Gracie had against these men, Phylly had no idea, but knowing Gracie, it would only be a matter of time before she found out.

'Jimmy, this is Benedict and Roberto,' Florrie said, introducing the two POWs, who had stopped hoeing and were smiling warmly at him.

'*Buongiorno*, Jimmy,' Benedict said.

Jimmy stared at them both, surprised at what he saw. He hadn't expected them to look so normal, and so cheerful. Florrie had told him about them arriving while he ate his breakfast.

'Hello,' he said quietly, suddenly overcome with shyness.

'I have three *bambini*.' Benedict put his hand in his

jacket pocket and pulled out a photo, holding it out for Jimmy and Florrie to look. 'Marco, Alberto and Elena.' He pointed to each child as he named them. 'My wife, Maddalena.'

'You must miss them,' Florrie said.

Benedict shrugged. '*Si.* My wife happy I safe now, out of war. We write letters and I go home one day. Jimmy, how old you?'

'Eleven,' Jimmy said.

Benedict beamed. 'Like Marco.'

'Would you like a drink?' Florrie offered the two men bottles of cold tea.

'*Grazie.*' They opened the bottles and took long, appreciative drinks.

'Have any spare for me?' Phylly asked, coming over to them, her hoe balanced over her shoulder.

'Of course,' Florrie handed her a bottle out of the basket

'Morning, Jimmy,' Phylly smiled at him. 'Did you sleep well?'

'Yes, thank you.' He'd slept so well that he hadn't

woken up till gone nine o'clock when everyone else had already had their breakfast and started work.

'Good. Remember what we said about strawberries last night – would you like to pick some later on?'

Jimmy nodded. He'd already seen the field of strawberry plants, as Florrie had given him a guided tour round the farm. She'd shown him Jacob and Ned planting seeds in the greenhouses, lots of neat rows of fruit and vegetables growing, the hens and the cockerel who strutted about keeping an eye on his charges, and the beehives clustered at the end of the orchard. Florrie had warned him to keep away from them if he didn't want to get stung.

'You can go strawberry picking this afternoon, Jimmy,' Florrie said. 'Bea's taking you down to the Post Office before dinner, so you can post your letter home. We don't want Aunt Min worrying about where you are.'

Jimmy felt a warm glow in his stomach. Everyone was taking such good care of him, making him feel wanted, and he knew that Aunt Min would be pleased.

*

Late Sunday afternoon and the sun was slanting down into the sheltered garden at the back of the farmhouse. The air was fragrant with the heady smell of the climbing roses which clambered up the surrounding walls, their blossoms spilling down in swathes of dusky pink.

Phylly loved the little walled garden, where the grass was scattered with white daisies and there was a gentle background hum of bees visiting the colourful tapestry of flowers. Sitting on a rug on the grass, she closed her eyes, leaned back on her arms and relaxed, listening to the hubbub of conversation going on around her.

'Thank you for the delicious tea,' Edwin said. 'I haven't had such a good home-cooked meal since I came to England. I sure appreciate you inviting me.'

'You're welcome,' Bea said. 'And you didn't need to bring gifts, but it was very kind of you.'

'It's my pleasure. I can see they're being enjoyed.'

Phylly knew he must be referring to Jimmy, who'd been sitting cross-legged on the grass, engrossed in one of the comics that Edwin had brought him, ever since they'd all come out to the garden after finishing tea.

Comics, Hershey chocolate bars and gum weren't the only things Edwin had brought with him. Arriving punctually at three o'clock, dressed in his smart American uniform, he'd brought cans of peaches and meat, some sugar and a precious bar of perfumed soap. Everyone knew the American forces weren't rationed the way the British people were, but they generously shared what they had.

'Will you be flying tomorrow?' Gracie asked.

'I'm not sure,' Edwin said. 'You said that your husband's a navigator like me?'

'Yes, on Lancasters, but he doesn't tell me much,' she paused. 'You know about what it's like up there on an op. He doesn't want to talk about it, but I'd like to know so I can try to understand what it's like for him.'

'Well ... it's different for us because we're flying in the daytime, but one thing for sure that'll be the same is it's always cold up there, real cold. We wear heated suits to keep us warm, and the air's too thin, so we're on oxygen masks ... ' He stopped. 'Are you OK, Gracie?'

Phylly opened her eyes and looked at her friend, whose face had gone pale and her eyes were bright with tears. Her husband had been right not to tell her, Phylly thought; he knew Gracie so well and for all her bravado of wanting to know, it really was best that she didn't.

'They look after all the flyers well, don't they?' Phylly said, catching Edwin's eye.

He looked gratefully at her and nodded. 'They sure do – a great breakfast before we go, doughnuts and hot coffee when we get back. I'm sure it's the same for your husband, though maybe not the doughnuts.'

'Have you been to London yet?' Phylly asked, steering the conversation onto safer ground. 'Jimmy told me he's seen lots of American servicemen there.'

Edwin shook his head. 'No, not yet. I've spent all my free time here in Norfolk. I've been looking for somewhere and it's taken a while to find.' He smiled. 'Not having any signposts up makes it kinda hard for a stranger to find their way around.'

'Have you found it yet?' Florrie asked from where she was sitting on the old wooden bench next to Bea.

'I hope so.' Edwin put his hand inside his pocket and pulled out his wallet. Opening it, he took out something, then stood up from where he was sitting on the grass, walked across and handed it to Bea. 'I was hoping you might be able to help me with this.'

Bea looked at what he'd given her and gasped, putting her hand to her mouth as her face drained of colour. Swallowing hard, she looked up at Edwin and in a shaky voice asked, 'How did you get this?'

Chapter Three

'My mom gave it me before I came overseas,' Edwin said.

Bea frowned. 'Your mother? But how did she get this?'

From where Phylly sat on the grass, she could see that Edwin had given Bea a photograph.

'It's a picture of her with her best friend, she took it with her when she left England.' He smiled at Bea. 'I think that's you standing next to my mom. Is that right?'

'You're Annie's boy?' Bea stared at Edwin, studying his face as if she were looking for traces of her friend.

'I never even knew she had a son . . . ' Bea's voice wavered, and she took a few moments to compose herself, dashing away tears with her knuckle. 'This is such a surprise . . . after all these years . . . '

'Yes, Annie's my mom.' Edwin knelt down in front of Bea and gently laid his hand on her arm. 'I'm real sorry I shocked you, I didn't intend to upset you.'

Bea put her hand on his. 'No, don't be sorry, I'm glad you're here.' She smiled. 'I can't tell you how much this means to me. After Annie suddenly stopped writing, I never thought I'd ever hear anything of her again, and now here you are . . . her grown-up son.'

'She asked me to try and find you, to see how you are and tell you that she's sorry for disappearing. She's never forgotten you.'

'I've never forgotten her either,' Bea said softly.

'Can we look at the photograph?' Gracie asked, getting up and going to stand behind Bea.

'Of course,' Bea said.

Phylly joined Gracie as Bea pointed to the taller of the two women, who stood arm in arm, beaming at the camera, both of them were wearing the longer-style skirts, smart long-sleeved blouses and hats of earlier years. 'That's Annie, and this is me.'

Phylly recognised Bea – she hadn't changed very much.

'Where was the photograph taken?' Gracie asked.

'At the summer fete, at Lawton Hall Auxiliary Hospital, where we both worked,' Bea explained. 'During the last summer of the Great War.'

'Where's Annie now?' Florrie asked.

'Back home in the United States, in Maine.'

'But she went to live in Canada,' Bea said.

'That's right, but she had to move,' Edwin said. 'Before I was born.'

'I recall your father being adamant that *he* wouldn't live anywhere else except Canada, so Annie *had* to go and live there when they married,' Bea said. 'I'm surprised he changed his mind.'

'He didn't.' Edwin sat back down on the grass before continuing. 'I don't know the full story because my mom wouldn't ever tell me, all I know is that when she arrived in Canada it didn't turn out like she hoped it would. He wasn't a good husband to her, and when she found out she was expecting me, she was frightened for her unborn child, so she ran away.'

Bea gasped. 'Poor Annie.'

'It must have been real hard for her, but my mom's a strong woman and she found herself a job, had me and brought me up.'

'Wasn't Annie's married name Sinclair? Yours is Johnson,' Florrie said. 'Did your mother marry again?'

'No, ma'am, she's never remarried. She was frightened my father would find her, so she changed her name when she ran away, used her mother's maiden name. She heard he'd died a while back.'

'Why didn't she just come home?' Ned said. He'd been watching and listening as Edwin had revealed who he was but hadn't spoken until now. He picked up the photograph from Bea's lap and stared at it.

'I asked her the same thing, but all she said was she was too ashamed and too stubborn to go back.'

Ned shook his head. 'She always was stubborn, right

from a little girl. Annie and Bea were as thick as thieves right from when they first went to school. They were always together.'

'Annie used to spend more time here at Catchetts than she did at her own home,' Florrie added. 'She should have come home, though. How did she manage on her own? How'd she earn a living?'

'Cooking. My mom's a great cook and she eventually opened up her own diner – she's her own boss.'

'I wish she'd come home,' Ned said gruffly, his face pale and drawn. 'We'd have helped her.' He thrust the photograph back into Bea's hand and, without waiting for any response, turned and went back into the farmhouse.

Phylly noticed Bea and Florrie glance at each other, an unspoken message passing between them. Had something happened that they weren't saying? Why was Ned so upset?

'Do you have any other family living in the village?' Gracie asked.

'I don't think so. I've asked around at the village shop

but they said my mom's mom, my grandmother, had died,' Edwin said.

'That's right, a couple of years after your mother went to Canada,' Florrie said. 'There wasn't anyone else. Annie's father was dead, and she was an only child.'

'I wish Annie had told me,' Bea said, sadly. 'Her letters never hinted that anything was wrong. Her new life in Canada sounded wonderful and she wrote about what a good husband Joe was. Did he hurt her?' Bea bit her lip. 'Was she in danger?'

Edwin shrugged. 'All she's told me was that he used to drink a lot, and sometimes when men have too much they can get handy with their fists. It must have been something like that if she was scared for her baby.'

Florrie sighed, shaking her head. 'You know what they say: marry in haste . . . '

'Could you tell me about how my parents met and married?' Edwin asked. 'I know it didn't work out, but I'd still like to find out. Mom would never talk about it.'

'Your father, Joe, was a patient at the Auxiliary Hospital where Annie and I both worked in the kitchens doing the cooking,' Bea explained. 'We didn't have much to do with the patients while they were bed-bound on the ward, but once they were mobile and allowed out into the gardens, we sometimes saw them.'

'Is that where they met? In the garden?' Edwin asked.

'Yes, not long after this photograph was taken. They took a liking to each other and grabbed every chance they could to see each other. Annie fell in love with him and his tales of life in Canada. She hadn't known him that long when he proposed.'

'How long?' Edwin said.

Bea thought for a moment. 'It was less than three months from them first meeting to getting married. Probably too soon, but she was twenty-one, so old enough to make up her own mind.'

'Her mother and I told her she should wait,' Florrie added. 'But she wouldn't listen.'

'They married just before your father was sent back to Canada and Annie followed him a few months later.'

Edwin nodded, taking in all that Bea had told him. 'Thank you for telling me, I appreciate it. I got lucky being based here in Norfolk and had been trying to find you every chance I got.' He smiled. 'That night I found Phylly and Jimmy in the ditch, I was on my way here. I'd finally tracked the village down and was going to ask directions to Catchetts Farm. It was a twist of fate that brought me here with them.'

'Why didn't you tell us who you were when you brought them home?' Florrie asked.

Edwin shrugged. 'It wasn't the right time – you needed to settle Jimmy in, my news could wait a while longer.'

'Well, now you've found us, I hope you'll keep visiting,' Florrie said. 'Your mother felt at home here and I hope you will too.'

Edwin smiled. 'Thank you, ma'am, I'd be glad to come visit. I'll write my mom as soon as I get back to base, tell her I found you and gave you her message.'

'I'm glad you did,' Bea said. 'Do you think Annie would like me to write to her?'

'She sure would.'

*

Phylly had shooed the last of the stragglers into the hen coop and shut them in safely for the night, and was on her way back to the farmhouse when she spotted Ned leaning on the gate of the water meadow. He was staring out towards where Florrie's cow, Nancy, the pretty little Jersey with the melting chocolate eyes, was grazing the lush grass, rhythmically swishing her tail from side to side against the flies.

'It's a beautiful sunset.' Phylly joined Ned, leaning her arms on the top of the gate and looking up at the sky, which was streaked with apricot-coloured clouds.

Ned looked at her, startled. 'Beg your pardon?'

'I was just admiring the sunset.' Phylly paused. 'Are you all right, Ned?'

'Just lost in my thoughts for a while . . . thinking about the past.' He pulled off his cap and rubbed his hand over his eyes. 'Hearing about Edwin's mother, Annie . . . it's got me thinking it over again.'

'Edwin being her son was a big surprise for you all.'

He nodded. 'I'm glad he's come to see us, but I'm shocked about what happened to Annie.' He paused, lost in his thoughts for a few moments, twisting his cap round in his hands. 'I always thought she was happy and that made it easier ... but knowing what really happened ...' Ned sighed. 'If I'd known what was going on, I'd have gone over there and brought her home myself.'

'She didn't want anyone here to know what had happened – perhaps she was ashamed and regretted marrying so quickly.'

'Annie never was any good at admitting she was wrong, but with a baby on the way ...' Ned shook his head. 'She should have swallowed her foolish stubbornness and written to us.'

'Annie *did* take her child away from danger.' Phylly said. 'It couldn't have been easy for her moving to another country where she didn't know anyone and had no one to help her.'

They fell into silence, looking out over the meadow where swallows were skimming over the wildflowers, hawking for insects to feed their ever-hungry young, who hung over the sides of their mud nests in the barns.

Phylly breathed in deeply, appreciating the delicate scent of honeysuckle perfuming the evening air from where it grew over the gate posts.

'I wanted to marry her,' Ned suddenly announced, keeping his eyes firmly fixed on the sky, which was changing moment by moment, the apricot blending into lilac.

Phylly stared at Ned. 'She didn't jilt you for the Canadian, did she?'

'No, no, Annie would never have done that.' Ned's gaze met Phylly's. 'She didn't know how I felt. I never told her because I was waiting to see if I survived the war first, then I was going to tell her. Too many of my friends had been killed, leaving their sweethearts and wives behind, so I thought the best thing to do was wait and see if I survived. If I did, then I'd tell her how I felt, ask her to be my girl,' he paused, 'and then maybe my wife. Only I left it too late. By the time I came home after the war, she was married.'

'I'm sure if she'd known . . .'

Ned shrugged. 'Maybe not. A Canadian soldier was

probably more exciting than a Tommy. None of that matters now, it's the past, but I'm sorry it turned out badly for her.'

'What about you?' Phylly asked. 'Did you never find someone else?'

Ned drew in a deep breath. 'No, she was the one for me and I left it too late . . . ' He shrugged.

Phylly touched his arm. 'I'm sorry. It must be hard to hear how things worked out for her.'

Ned nodded. 'I wish she'd written and told us, I would have helped her. All water under the bridge now, though.' He looked up at the sky where the colours had faded down to the horizon, and the last rays of sunlight tinted the clouds before the dipped far below the horizon. 'Looks like the weather's set fine for tomorrow.' Ned put on his cap and smiled at Phylly. 'You and young Jimmy can pick some more strawberries, he's getting quite a taste for them.'

'*O sole, o sole mio*,' Phylly and Jimmy sang together.

'*Bene, bene*,' Roberto clapped, beaming at them.

'Very good,' Benedict said. 'You learn well.'

The two Italian POWs had settled well into life at Catchetts Farm since their arrival two weeks ago and had been teaching Phylly and Jimmy part of the Italian song which they often sang as they worked.

'I love your language,' Phylly said. '"*Sole*" sounds so much nicer than just plain "sun".'

Benedict smiled. '*Si*, is a beautiful language. You like Italia too, I think. You go there one day when war is done.'

'I'd like that,' Phylly said.

Talking of visiting Italy made Phylly think of how Gracie had spoken warmly of her travels there. She glanced over to where her friend was picking peas further over the field. If only Gracie would get over what was bothering her and get to know Benedict and Roberto, she'd be able to talk to them about Italy, but she never got involved with them, only spoke to them when she had to and kept her distance emotionally and physically.

'What did you do in the army?' Jimmy asked. 'Did you fly in planes like Edwin?'

'No,' Benedict said, 'Me and Roberto were cooks. We make food.'

Jimmy stared at them. 'Cooks!'

'*Si*, cooks,' Benedict replied. 'We no fight.'

'Sounds like a good job to me,' Phylly said. 'An army marches on its stomach, so they say. Right – Jimmy, Benedict and Roberto, can you take the full baskets of pea pods back to the yard and empty them out for me, please?'

'*Si*.' Benedict and Roberto both picked up two baskets each and Jimmy took one, and together the three of them headed the short distance back to the farmyard.

'We should have time to fill up the baskets again before it's time to stop for dinner,' Phylly called over to Gracie.

'If you can find the time when you're not singing,' Gracie snapped back.

Phylly drew in a sharp breath. 'It helps pass the time while we work. You'd enjoy it if you joined in.'

'Humph!' Gracie snorted.

Phylly threw down the pea plant she was stripping

of pea pods and stomped over to Gracie. 'What *is* the matter with you? Why are you being like this?'

Gracie stared at her, her brown eyes unblinking. 'What do you mean?'

'Oh, come on, Gracie.' Phylly said, throwing her arms wide. 'You know exactly what I mean. Whenever we're working near Benedict or Roberto you go all funny. Aloof, haughty, distant . . . cold, is that enough to explain it? I've never known you behave like this to anyone before, but you've been downright unpleasant to Benedict and Roberto since they arrived on the farm.'

'I'm polite,' Gracie said throwing a handful of pea pods into her basket.

'Barely. Look, I've had enough of this. Everyone else on this farm has welcomed them and appreciates how hard they work, and what a help they've been, but you . . . ' Phylly sighed. 'Just tell me why you don't like them, because that's clearly how it looks.'

'They're the enemy,' Gracie stood up straight and crossed her arms. 'You're all hobnobbing with the enemy.'

Phylly stared at her friend, whose face was set hard, her lips pressed together in a thin line and a sheen of tears glossing her eyes. She reached out and put her hand on Gracie's arm. 'They're prisoners of war and out of it.'

'But they're still the enemy – our men died fighting people like them, and are *still* dying.'

'Not against the Italians. They surrendered last year, remember.' Phylly paused. 'Benedict and Roberto are just ordinary people – they didn't even want to go in the army, but had to, then all they did was cook meals. Roberto's just a boy, he's only a few years older than Jimmy.'

Gracie didn't say anything, but a single tear trickled down her face, leaving a tell-tale track in the smudged dirt on her cheek.

'Most of the men involved in the war don't want to fight,' Phylly said, putting her arm around Gracie. 'They're only in it because stupid politicians do crazy things and get their countries involved in war, then sit back in safety while innocent men have to go out and fight.'

'Like Richard,' Gracie's voice was hoarse.

'Yes, like Richard and Edwin, and Roberto and Benedict before they were captured.'

'I keep thinking . . . ' Gracie chewed on her bottom lip, 'that Richard is risking his life to fight against the enemy, people like them, and I'm worrying myself sick about it.' Her voice wobbled. 'Every night I lie awake wondering if he's up there, is he safe . . . '

'I know,' Phylly squeezed Gracie's shoulders. 'I know how much you worry.'

'Last night was a bomber's moon, did you see it?'

Phylly nodded. She'd woken in the night and seen Gracie sitting by the window, staring up at the moonlit sky on one of her night-time vigils.

'How do you think Richard would treat our POWs, would he cold-shoulder them?'

Gracie shrugged Phylly's arm off. 'You don't understand what it's like!'

'I do,' Phylly said. 'I understand all too well.'

'I can't—' Gracie said.

'Then you're missing out.'

'*O sole mio* . . .' The sound of singing made Phylly turn around to see that Jimmy and the POWs were coming in through the field gate with the empty baskets.

'They're back.' She turned and met Gracie's gaze. 'Please think about what I've said.'

Gracie shook her head.

Phylly gently touched her friend's shoulder and headed back to where the others had started picking peas again. Glancing back, she saw that Gracie was staring down at the ground, wiping tears away from her face. How was she going to get Gracie to overcome her prejudice and accept Benedict and Roberto for who they were, genuinely nice people and not the enemy?

'You're doing a good job there,' Jacob said. 'When I'm on parade tonight the Captain'll be able to see his face in that boot.'

Jimmy smiled at Jacob, who was sitting beside him on the wall just outside the farmhouse, polishing the other one of his boots while Ned sat the other side working on his own. Both men had changed into their khaki Home Guard uniform and were getting ready to go on duty.

'Did you really find these boots on the washing line?' Jimmy asked as he buffed the leather toe with the boot brush just as Jacob had shown him. 'Florrie told me, but she was joking really, wasn't she?'

Jacob laughed. 'No. It's the honest truth. They were there one morning, tied up in a pair by the laces and dangling over the washing line. There'd been a bombing raid on Norwich in the night, so they must have fallen out of a German plane or been thrown out when a crew bailed out.' He held up the boot he was working on to admire and added, 'They're good ones too. The best I've ever had and a perfect fit.'

The three of them fell into silence for a few minutes as they polished.

'Did you like pea-picking today, Jimmy?' Ned asked.

'Yes. I've done some before with Aunt Min; she grows peas in her garden, but not as many as you do.' Jimmy thought about the garden back in London, where he and Aunt Min had worked together growing vegetables to add to their rations. They'd fitted in as much as they could into the small plot, but their row of peas had been tiny in comparison to the amount grown here at Catchetts. If Aunt Min could see the field of peas she'd be amazed.

Jimmy missed Aunt Min and wished she would come and visit. Every time he wrote to her, he asked her when she was coming to see him, and she always replied 'soon', but never exactly when. He hadn't had a letter from her for a few days now and that worried him. Was she all right? Was she safe? With the doodlebugs landing on London it wasn't a safe place to be. Jimmy stopped polishing and sighed.

'Are you all right?' Ned asked.

Jimmy hung his head to hide the tears that suddenly stung his eyes. 'I'm worried about Aunt Min.' His voice sounded hoarse and he swallowed hard to try and relieve the tightness that was squeezing his throat. 'I'm scared she'll get hit by a doodlebug.'

Ned put a hand on Jimmy's shoulder. 'I'm sure she'll be all right. She got through the Blitz, didn't she?'

Jimmy nodded and raised his gaze to meet Ned's. 'We used to shelter in the Underground, sleep there all night sometimes. But there's no air raid warning with the doodlebugs, no chance to shelter.'

Thinking of them made Jimmy shiver. He hated the way they came buzzing through the air like angry wasps, making everyone stop and hold their breath, listening for the engine to cut out. All you could do was wait. Hope and pray it would miss you. Wait for the roar and flash to come from somewhere else. If it did, then you knew you'd survived. That time. No one knew when they'd come next or where they'd fall, which was why Aunt Min had sent him away to safety. She should have come with him. He'd lost his dad because of Hitler's war – he'd been sent to the bottom of the Atlantic by a German submarine – and he didn't want to lose Aunt Min as well. He worried about her in the long hours in middle of the night, the terror of what might happen to her gnawing away at his stomach.

A wave of fury raced through Jimmy. He wished he

could do something to stop the war – he'd go and fight if he could.

'I wish I could join the Home Guard,' Jimmy said. 'I will as soon as I'm old enough.'

'I hope the war will be long over by then,' Jacob said easing his foot into his shining boot and starting to tie the laces. 'It can't go on much longer, now our boys are back in France.'

'You're doing your bit to help here on the farm, Jimmy,' Ned said. 'I'm sure your Aunt Min'll come and visit soon and she'll be really pleased to see how well you've settled in, you'll see.'

Jimmy hoped Ned was right. All he could do for now was hope and pray that Aunt Min was safe. And that she kept safe, no matter how many rockets fell on London.

'Would you look at that rooster go,' Edwin laughed as they stood watching Winston round up a gaggle of his hens who'd strayed too far from him towards the end of the orchard. His chest was puffed up and his glorious bottle-green curled tail feathers bobbed around as he dashed this way and that.

'Rooster? Winston's a cockerel,' Phylly said. She and Jimmy were walking around the farm on Saturday afternoon, giving Edwin a guided tour as he hadn't had a chance to look over the farm on his previous two visits. 'You Americans speak a strange type of English.'

'I could say the same for you guys,' Edwin said. 'You call a vest a waistcoat.'

Jimmy laughed. 'Vests are for keeping out the cold. And they itch.'

'There's a bunch of differences between our two countries,' Edwin said. 'Did you know that when each one of us "Yanks" arrives here, we're given a book to help us understand more about Britain. We don't want to get things wrong and offend you good people.'

'How?' Phylly asked.

Edwin grinned. 'Lots of ways,' he paused to consider for a moment. 'One important thing to remember is that you drive on the other side of the road – several of the guys I know have forgotten that sometimes. Then there's your money.' Edwin shook his head. 'I got in such a muddle to start with trying to figure it out. There's so many different coins: the farthings, shillings, pennies, sixpences, florins, half crowns.' He shrugged. 'And you need to know how many of each fit into each other. It's taken me a while to get my head around it. American money is so much easier.'

'What do you like about England?' Jimmy asked, folding his arms across his chest.

'Well . . . let me try and think of something . . .' Edwin teased. He paused, scratching his head as if he were thinking hard, then grinned, his sea-blue eyes twinkling. 'I've thought of something – the real friendly people, the beautiful countryside, and the history. I sure love all the old buildings. Our ones back home are nowhere near as old as yours. I've been to see the cathedral in Norwich—'

Jimmy laughed loudly. 'It's Norwich, it rhymes with porridge, not "Nor witch".'

Edwin shrugged and grinned. 'I know that now, though I didn't when I first went there. I soon learned.'

'Have you been inside the cathedral?' Phylly asked. She was enjoying watching how well Edwin and Jimmy got on. Edwin's friendly, cheerful manner and genuine kindness had made him and Jimmy firm friends in the short time they'd known each other.

'I sure have. It's incredible to think that it's eight hundred years old. I've been in Norwich castle too. I love all the village churches, they're so old and it makes you shiver thinking how many people have sat in those places going back hundreds of years.'

'I've never thought of it like that,' Phylly said. 'It's just normal in England. We grow up with these buildings around us.'

'It's one of the things my mom misses about England.'

'If you like, we could show you the old abbey ruins in the next village,' Phylly offered. 'And there's a ruined castle not far away as well.'

Edwin smiled. 'I sure would like that. We should plan a visit to them.'

'Do you miss America?' Jimmy asked as they turned and started walking back to the house, where

Florrie had promised them some freshly baked scones and jam.

'I miss my mom, of course, and her apple pie, and the special holiday days like Christmas, Fourth of July and Thanksgiving. We celebrate them here, of course, but it's not the same as being back home with your folks.'

'You could come and celebrate them with us,' Phylly said. 'Well, the ones we have – we don't do Thanksgiving or Fourth of July.'

'What's Thanksgiving?' Jimmy asked.

'It's when we remember the first Thanksgiving – when the Pilgrims celebrated their first harvest in the New World. It's always the fourth Thursday in November. We have turkey, mashed potato, cranberry sauce, pumpkin pie . . . ' Edwin paused and then smiled. 'Maybe you could all come and celebrate at the base this coming Thanksgiving.'

'There you are,' Gracie called, coming over to them. 'Florrie sent me to tell you the scones are ready, and if you don't come quick, Jacob and Ned will eat the lot.'

'We can't have that, can we?' Phylly linked her arms

through Jimmy's and Edwin's and hurried them back to the farmhouse.

Florrie's freshly baked scones had been reduced to just a few crumbs and everyone was lingering around the scrubbed wooden kitchen table enjoying the light-hearted chatter. Jimmy sat at one end, engrossed in another comic that Edwin had brought him.

'Oh, nearly forgot,' Florrie said, getting up from where she sat near Jacob, going across to the dresser and taking something out of a drawer. 'I remembered we'd got this photograph.' She handed it to Edwin, 'I thought you might be interested in seeing it.'

'Thank you.' Edwin took the photo and looked at it.

From Phylly's seat beside him she could see it was an old school photograph, taken some time ago by the look of the children, the girls dressed in white pinafores and the boys with stiff-looking white collars.

Bea got up from her seat and came to stand beside Edwin. 'I'd forgotten about this. Do you recognise anyone on there?'

'Is my mom on there?' Edwin hovered his finger over each child, looking for his mother. 'This one?'

'Yes, and that's me beside her,' Bea pointed out. 'And there's Ned in the back row.'

Edwin smiled. 'I'm real glad to see this. I've never seen a picture of Mom as a child. Is this at the village school?'

'Yes, the same one that's still there now, where Jimmy will go in September.'

Hearing his name, Jimmy looked up and pulled a face at the mention of school.

'You're not keen on school?' Edwin asked.

Jimmy shook his head.

'Well, it's a lot better than the one I went to,' Gracie said. 'At least you get to come home every day. I was there for months on end. I'd never send a child of mine to boarding school. If Richard and I have children they'll go to a day school.'

'Didn't you—' Jimmy began but stopped at the sound of a loud knocking on the door.

'I'll go.' Phylly got up from the table and went

to answer the door, but her stomach dropped as she opened it and saw who was standing on the doorstep. It was the boy from the Post Office, and clutched in his hand was one of the dreaded buff-yellow envelopes. A telegram. No one wanted one of those, because too often the news they brought wasn't welcome.

'For Mrs Templeman,' he said, holding it out.

Phylly took it and scanned the name on the front, checking it carefully in case there'd been a mistake, but it was written clearly in black ink. The telegram was for Gracie.

Chapter Four

Phylly watched the telegram boy ride out of the yard as fast as he could on his too-large bicycle. He probably disliked delivering telegrams as much people disliked receiving them, and if he could, departed before the news he'd delivered hit home.

It could be good news for Gracie, Phylly thought – perhaps Richard was coming to see her . . . or it could be bad news . . . a telegram in wartime wasn't so welcome. Phylly stared at the innocent-looking envelope. Was it bad news in here? There was only one way to find out.

She paused outside the door for a moment, listening to the sound of laughter coming from the kitchen. Gracie was in full flow, telling one of her funny tales about boarding school. Closing her eyes, Phylly sent up a silent prayer that whatever news the telegram brought, it wouldn't blow her friend's happiness away.

Bracing herself with a deep breath, she stepped into the kitchen. The laughter rapidly died when those sitting facing her spotted the telegram in her hands.

Gracie, sitting with her back to Phylly, carried on talking. 'The last midnight feast we had was . . .' She suddenly stopped and, following the gazes of those sitting opposite her, turned to look at Phylly, her face blanching white when her eyes locked on to the buff-yellow envelope.

'It's a telegram.' Phylly knew she was stating the obvious.

Without waiting to be told it was for her, Gracie shoved her chair backwards, making a spine-shivering scraping sound against the tiled floor, rushed over to Phylly and snatched the telegram out of her hand. All the colour drained away from Gracie's face as she read her name on the front, and without uttering a single sound, she strode across the room, flung open the hall door and pounded up the stairs.

'Gracie,' a chorus of voices called after her.

Phylly went to follow her, but Florrie grabbed her arm. 'Give her a few minutes.'

She nodded. 'It's probably Richard letting her know that he's coming to visit.' Her voice sounded hollow to her own ears.

'Let's hope so,' Bea said.

A loud wail from upstairs gave them their answer. It wasn't good news. Phylly was out of the kitchen and up the stairs in seconds, barging into the room she and Gracie shared, where she found her friend lying face down on the bed, her body heaving with sobs. The telegram lay abandoned on the floor.

'Gracie!' Phylly knelt down beside the bed, putting her arm around Gracie's shoulders. 'What's happened?'

'Richard's—' Gracie's hoarse voice was muffled as she spoke into the eiderdown. 'I can't . . . you read it.'

Phylly retrieved the telegram from the floor and read the words with a sinking heart.

REGRET TO INFORM YOU THAT YOUR
HUSBAND 74812 F/SGT RICHARD
TEMPLEMAN IS REPORTED MISSING AS
THE RESULT OF AIR OPERATIONS ON 12TH
AUGUST 1944 STOP LETTER FOLLOWS STOP
ANY FURTHER INFORMATION RECEIVED
WILL BE IMMEDIATELY COMMUNICATED
TO YOU STOP

'Oh, Gracie.' Phylly laid the telegram on the bedside cabinet which separated their two beds. 'I'm so sorry,' she squeezed her friend's hand. 'I know it's really hard, but you must keep thinking positively. Richard is missing. His plane might have landed somewhere else or he bailed out.'

A fresh wave of sobs heaved through Gracie and she shook her head. 'He's gone . . . I know he is.'

'You don't know that, no one does.' Phylly took in

a sharp breath, trying to ignore the hard knot in the pit of her stomach. She understood exactly how Gracie felt. Bracing herself, she spoke gently. 'All we can do is wait and hope. There's always hope, Gracie. Don't give up on that.'

Until they heard otherwise that's what they had to cling onto: hope, there was always hope.

'Will Gracie be OK?' Edwin asked, pushing his bicycle as he walked beside Phylly.

'I hope so.' Phylly was accompanying Edwin as far as the end of the farm lane on his way back to his base. She was glad to be outside after the oppressive mood in her and Gracie's bedroom. Florrie had brought a cup of sweet tea up for Gracie and insisted that Phylly go down and have one herself, saying that she would stay and keep Gracie company. After drinking her own cup of too-sweet tea, a waste of precious sugar ration, Phylly had thought, Bea had shooed her outside to get some fresh air.

'She's convinced Richard's not coming back, but

she's got to hope he will.' Phylly sighed. 'Until she hears different, there's still a chance that he's alive somewhere. I know it's hard, I understand how she feels . . . ' Phylly's voice cracked as a wave of painful memories shot through her.

'Phylly?' Edwin stopped walking and turned to her. 'What's wrong?'

'Nothing,' Phylly shook her head, sniffing back threatening tears. 'The telegram . . . it's just prodded an old wound, but I'm fine, honestly.'

Edwin laid a hand on her arm. 'If you don't mind me saying so, you don't look it.'

His kind words made it harder to hold back the tears that were making the world swirl and blur before her eyes. Phylly bit her bottom lip and gave herself a few moments to compose herself.

'I lost my fiancé at Dunkirk.' She shrugged. 'I've accepted it now, but sometimes when things like this happen, it's there again – remembering how it feels, the waiting for news, the pain . . . '

'Gee, I'm so sorry.' Edwin squeezed her arm.

'Thank you.' Phylly managed a wobbly smile and looked up, trying to spot the skylark which was singing its beautiful song somewhere overhead, giving herself time to gather herself together. 'I'm not the only person who's lost someone in this war, and the terrible thing is there'll be plenty more before it's over. I hope for Gracie's sake that Richard is one of the lucky ones and comes home.'

'Me, too.'

'So,' Phylly tried hard to make her voice sound positive, 'when are you coming to visit us again? Soon, I hope.'

'Is that an invitation?' Edwin grinned.

'You already have an open invitation from Florrie, you don't have to ask to come.'

'Then I'll see you all again real soon, as soon as I can get away. I'd better get going, I've a ten-mile ride ahead of me.'

'Mind how you go, especially round corners,' Phylly said, her gaze meeting his striking blue eyes.

'I always do, now. Take care, Phylly.'

Edwin launched himself on to his bicycle and

pedalled off, giving a final wave as he turned off the track and headed back to his base.

'Break-time,' Phylly called out at the welcome sight of Florrie and Jimmy coming into the field carrying the basket with their drinks and mid-morning snack.

She was working alongside Gracie and the two POWs, hoeing weeds out of swede plants, the hot sun making it thirsty work.

Leaving her hoe in the row to mark where she'd got to, Phylly started to follow Benedict and Roberto down to the gate where Florrie was waiting, and she glanced over to check if Gracie was coming too.

'Gracie, it's break-time,' Phylly called over to her. 'Time to stop.'

'I'm not hungry.' Gracie carried on chopping out the weeds around the small swede plants.

'But you didn't have any breakfast.' Stepping carefully across the rows of swedes, Phylly made her way over to her friend. She was worried because Gracie's healthy appetite had dwindled, and since she'd received the news about Richard more than a week ago, she'd been skipping breakfast altogether, just gulping down a cup of tea before rushing out to work. It wasn't the way to carry on when you were working hard on a farm and needed energy to keep going.

'I'm not *hungry*,' Gracie snapped.

'All right, but at least come and have a drink of cold tea.'

Gracie shrugged, dropped her hoe and allowed Phylly to link her arm into hers and lead her over to Florrie.

Benedict and Roberto had already got their drink and food and were sitting in the shade of the large oak tree in the hedge teaching Jimmy to carve shapes out of wood. The two Italians had a talent for turning bits of wood into intricate shapes, and Jimmy had apprenticed himself to them and was learning how to do it himself whenever he got the chance.

'Bread and jam?' Florrie held out a doorstep sandwich of her delicious bread with a ruby-red filling of strawberry jam to Gracie.

Gracie shook her head. 'No, thank you, Florrie, just some cold tea.' She took a bottle from the basket.

'Gracie! You need to eat,' Phylly said.

Gracie ignored her and without saying another word, headed off to sit in the shade further down the hedge away from where Jimmy and the POWs sat.

Phylly shook her head. 'She didn't have any breakfast again, so she must be hungry.'

'She looks pale and tired,' Florrie said, quietly. 'And so solemn – not like her normal self at all.'

'She's not sleeping much, either, just sits at the window looking out at the night.'

'Jacob and I wondered if it might be better for her if she went home for a bit, had a proper rest there.'

'I've already suggested that to her, but she'd rather stay here – she thinks her mother might be glad about Richard, and Gracie couldn't bear that. Remember how her mother was against her marrying Richard and would've stopped her if Gracie'd been under twenty-one. She wants to stay here with her friends and keep busy.'

Florrie sighed. 'That's a sad state when a girl can't go

home to her mother when she needs her. She must be a hard woman, from the stories Gracie's told us … and being sent away to school for months on end … '

'At least if she stays here we can look after her, as much as she'll let us,' Phylly said.

'We're all hoping for the best.' Florrie reached out and squeezed Phylly's arm and then looked up into the blue sky. 'Look at them,' she sighed, pointing to the white contrails crossing the blue, a frequent sight over Norfolk now, which showed the path of the American air force planes on their way to fight the enemy. 'All those young men up there, they're all someone's son, husband or father, going off to face goodness knows what … not knowing if they'll come home … men like Edwin … ' Florrie's voice wavered. She sniffed loudly and cleared her throat. 'If I could get my hands on that Hitler … if he came into my kitchen bossing me around, I'd soon sort him out. He's like a spoilt child stealing other children's toys, only he takes countries.'

Phylly put her arm around Florrie's shoulders. 'If you were in charge, there'd never be a war.'

Florrie nodded, patting Phylly's arm. 'We'll get through it. We did before. In the meantime, we must keep a good eye on those we've got close, including those young men,' she nodded towards the POWs, then picked up the basket. 'I'd best get on, Jacob and Ned'll be parched working in the greenhouses and be ready for their drink.'

Phylly joined Benedict, Roberto and Jimmy under the oak tree, where it felt deliciously cool under the spreading green leaves.

'What do you think?' Jimmy showed her his carving of a dog which he was whittling out of piece of wood under Benedict's careful tutoring.

'You're doing really well.' Phylly smiled. 'You'll soon be as good as Roberto.'

At the mention of his name, Roberto looked up from his work where he'd been deftly carving a shape out of the wood with his penknife. 'Is cat.'

'For guard, is present for his wife,' Benedict explained. 'Roberto sell his carvings to guards.'

'Do many of them buy them?' Jimmy asked.

Benedict bobbed his head. '*Si*, some.'

'Bet the one who brings you every day doesn't buy presents for people,' Jimmy said.

'No.' Benedict shook his head. 'He not good man. No *Italiano* like him.'

'I didn't like the look of him the first time I saw him.' Phylly remembered her first impression of him when he'd brought the POWs to the farm. 'Best keep out of his way, if you can.'

'I don't like him either,' Jimmy said. 'He always looks mean. Aunt Min would say he's like a dog that wants to bite you. Be careful near him.'

'Don't worry, we are,' Benedict reassured him. 'Very careful.'

'I'm nearly done, just a few more pins,' Bea said.

Jimmy kept completely still, watching as she turned the material over at the bottom of the new shirt he was trying on and pinned it into a hem.

'There, all done, if you slip it off carefully I can sew it up and then it's ready to wear.'

'Thank you.' Jimmy smiled at her – he liked spending time with Bea and watching her sew new clothes for him. She'd made this new shirt for him out of an unused tablecloth and he liked the blue material, its colour reminded him of the forget-me-nots that grew in the walled garden behind the farmhouse.

'My pleasure, I like making things for you.' Bea helped him take the shirt off. 'I'll get started on knitting you a new pullover next, the rate you're growing I think you'll need it by the time the weather turns colder.'

Dressed again in his old shirt and pullover, Jimmy settled himself on a chair beside Bea as she sat at the sewing machine instead of going outside. He liked to watch her sewing, fascinated as the needle bobbed up and down through the material.

'Benedict told me he mends the other Italian POWs' clothes for them when they get ripped doing work on the farms. He likes to sew, too,' Jimmy said.

'He's a good man.'

'Do you think they are happy to be here, in England?'

Bea stopped sewing and looked at him. 'I think if I

were them I'd rather be here than where there is fighting, wouldn't you?'

Jimmy nodded. 'But they miss their families.'

'I know, but at least they are safe.' Bea smiled. 'Lots of people aren't with their families because of the war. You're away from home, aren't you?'

'Yes, but I'm not a prisoner.'

'No, but I think Benedict and Roberto as are content as they can be away from their homes and families. They just have to wait until the war is over and then they can go home again. They seem all right to me – I think they enjoy coming here to work on the farm, they seem happy while they're here.'

'I think they are.'

Bea took hold of Jimmy's hand. 'What about you, Jimmy, are you happy here?'

He nodded. 'I like it here.'

'Good. Because I like having you here. Very much.' Bea smiled at him. 'How about if you finish sewing the hem on this shirt, then you can go and show Benedict what you've done?'

'Can I?'

'Yes, sit here.'

Jimmy sat on Bea's chair and listened carefully as she told him what to do.

'First of all, keep your fingers away from the needle, we don't want you sewn up – all you need to do is guide the material through. I'll turn the wheel, so you don't have to worry about that. All right?'

He nodded. Then, while he focused hard on the needle, material and keeping his fingers safe, Bea started to slowly turn the wheel and the needle began to dance up and down, stitching through the material as he guided the hem through underneath.

'That's it, you're doing it,' Bea said. 'Keep going.'

Phylly and Gracie were sitting outside on the low wall near the kitchen door, cleaning their brown Land Army-issue shoes, rubbing the polish into the worn leather to keep them in good order, as wearing them to work on the land took its toll.

'Jimmy and I are going to watch the barn owl

hunting over on the meadow later,' Phylly said. 'Would you like to come with us?'

Gracie shook her head. 'No, thanks.'

'Not even for a bit . . . ' Phylly began but paused at the sound of an engine coming down the lane towards the farm. Moments later a USAAF jeep drove into the farmyard – it was Edwin.

Bringing the jeep to a stop near them, he cut the engine and climbed out.

'Hi, there! Are you two setting up a shoe-shine business? If I'd known I could have brought a load over from the base for you.'

Phylly raised her eyebrows. 'Keeping our own shoes in good order is enough, thank you very much. So, what brings you over?'

'I've got a present for Bea.' Edwin picked up a box from the back seat of the jeep.

'I'll go and tell her you're here.' Gracie stood up and went inside.

'Has Gracie heard anything?' Edwin whispered.

Phylly shook her head. 'Nothing. No news is good

news, so they say . . . ' She sighed and stood up. 'Come on, let's go and give Bea her present.'

A few minutes later, everyone was gathered around the table watching Bea carefully unwrap the parcel.

'Is it really all the way from America?' Jimmy asked, his eyes shining as he watched Bea carefully unwrap the parcel and fold up the brown paper to reuse.

'It sure is.' Edwin smiled.

'Hurry up, Bea,' Jimmy said. 'It's exciting.'

Phylly nudged Jimmy. 'It's Bea's present, not yours.'

'It's all right, it's not every day we get a parcel arrive from America—' Bea gasped as she opened the box's lid. The inside was packed with things which had become scarce and hard to come by in rationed wartime Britain. She picked up a bar of soap, prettily wrapped in patterned paper, and smelt it. 'Oh, that's lovely, what a luxury.' She passed it to Florrie to have a smell.

'There's perfume and lipsticks!' Phylly said, peering into the open box. 'And stockings!'

The next few minutes were spent exclaiming in

delight over the contents of the box as Bea unpacked it and laid out the wonderful gifts on the kitchen table.

Phylly glanced over at Gracie who had remained quiet, keeping to the background, just watching what was going on but not joining in. The old Gracie would have dived in and been dancing around exclaiming at the wonderful luxuries. Seeing the change in her friend was hard, and the worst thing was that there was nothing Phylly could do to help her, because the fate of Richard wasn't in her hands.

'This is such a treat, Edwin,' Bea said, smiling at him. 'Annie knew just the things to send to give us all a boost. I'm sure she won't mind me sharing it out between us.' Bea chose two lipsticks and handed one each to Gracie and Phylly. 'These colours should look good on you both. I'm sure Dad, Ned and Jimmy will enjoy some of the chocolate.'

'Mom'll be delighted that you're all enjoying her gifts.' Edwin paused and then looked at Phylly and Gracie. 'This weekend we're gonna be celebrating the base's hundredth mission, and there's a dance on Saturday night – I wondered if you'd both like to come along as my guests. I'd come by and pick you up and bring home again afterward,' he smiled, 'and it would be a good opportunity to wear your new lipsticks.'

'A dance? I love dancing,' Phylly said. 'Thank you, I'd love to come. How about you, Gracie? It would be fun to dress up and go dancing wearing our new lipsticks.'

Gracie shook her head. 'No, thank you, Edwin. I appreciate your invitation, but I'm not in the mood for going dancing.'

'It's OK, I understand, but if you change your mind the invitation still holds good.'

The following evening, Phylly was washing up the plates after tea, while Jimmy and Bea dried the clean ones.

'Have you decided what you're going to wear to the dance on Saturday night?' Bea asked.

Phylly laughed. 'That's an easy choice because I've only got one dress. A bit of the hem's come down, so can I borrow your sewing machine to mend it please, Bea?'

'Of course, you can, I—' Bea paused and stared out of the kitchen window, her attention caught by a strange woman carrying a suitcase, who'd just walked into the farmyard. 'Who's that?'

Phylly and Jimmy stopped what they were doing and looked out of the window.

'Aunt Min!' Jimmy shrieked, dropping his teacloth and tearing out of the back door.

Phylly and Bea watched through the window as Jimmy ran across the farmyard and flung himself in his Aunt Min's open arms in a joyful reunion.

'Look at him, he's so happy to see his aunt again. Did you know she was coming, Bea?'

'No,' Bea's voice sounded pinched.

Phylly looked at Bea, who had an odd expression on her face. 'Are you all right?'

Bea bit her bottom lip. 'I hope she hasn't come to take him home again. London's not safe with all those rockets falling on it. Surely she wouldn't take him back to that, would she?'

*

Jimmy stepped back and looked up at his Aunt Min, taking in every detail of her, from her round glasses, which magnified her blue eyes, to the brown felt hat with its jaunty feather sticking out of the band around it. Seeing her here at Catchetts Farm was a miracle.

'Oh, it's good to see you again.' Aunt Min rested her hands on his shoulders. 'You look well and you've got roses in your cheeks.' She studied at him for a few moments. 'And I'm sure you've grown taller since you left London.'

'I didn't know you were coming,' Jimmy said.

She smiled warmly at him. 'I thought I'd surprise you.'

'It's the best surprise I've ever had.' Jimmy threw his arms around his aunt again and hugged her tightly and she squeezed him back.

Loosening her hold on him, Aunt Min said, 'Now are you going to take me in so I can meet all the people you tell me about in your letters?'

'They're going to be surprised to see you,' Jimmy said, taking hold of Aunt Min's hand and leading her towards the house.

Five minutes later, after Jimmy had proudly introduced Aunt Min to everyone, she was settled at the kitchen table with a cup of tea in front of her and some bread, butter and jam which Florrie had insisted she have.

'Oh, what lovely butter,' Aunt Min said appreciatively after taking her first bite. 'You don't get any like that in London these days.'

'Florrie makes it from the cream we get from Nancy – that's Florrie's cow,' Jimmy said.

'Jimmy's got the hang of milking,' Bea told Aunt Min. 'He's got such a gentle way with animals.'

Aunt Min put down her cup after taking a sip of tea. 'It's such a different world for him here, and good for him to be living out in the fresh air.' She looked at Jimmy fondly. 'I can see a change in him, he's filled out a bit and I'm sure he's grown taller – no wonder with food as good as this to eat.'

'Food rationing's not so bad on a farm,' Florrie said. 'It must be harder in the city.'

Aunt Min nodded. 'I do a lot of queuing for not a lot

of shopping, but the veg plot in my garden helps.' She glanced at her watch. 'Can you recommend a place to stay in the village? Only I don't want to leave it too late before I go and find a room. I had planned to find one as soon as I got off the bus, but I couldn't help myself, I had to come and see Jimmy first.'

'You don't need to do that,' Bea said. 'You can stay here with us. You'd see more of Jimmy that way.'

'You can sleep in my room, Aunt Min,' Jimmy said. 'I'll bed down on the settee in the parlour. That's all right, isn't it, Florrie?'

'Of course it is.' Florrie smiled. 'You're welcome to stay with us as long as you like.'

'Well, if you're sure, then thank you, I'd be delighted to stay here. It's very kind of you to put me up,' Aunt Min smiled. 'Jimmy's told me so much about the farm in his letters, so it'll be lovely to get to know it for myself.'

'That's settled, then.' Bea got up from the table. 'I'll go and sort the beds out. Jimmy, will you bring Aunt Min's case up for her?'

'Then can I show her around?' Jimmy asked.

'Course you can,' Florrie said, 'just let your aunt finish her tea first.'

Halfway through Jimmy's guided tour around the farm, just as they reached the orchard, Aunt Min caught hold of his arm. 'Can we sit down a minute? My old legs aren't as young as yours and I need a breather.'

Jimmy had noticed Aunt Min had been puffing a bit as they'd walked. 'Are you feeling all right? Are you ill?'

She swatted the idea away with her hand. 'Just need to stop for a minute and get me breath back, that's all . . . you've hurried me around looking at everything . . . and I've had a long day.'

Jimmy steered her over to sit on a wooden crate, and they sat side by side watching the chickens searching for insects in the long grass for a few minutes before Aunt Min turned to him and asked, 'Are you happy here, Jimmy? Really happy?'

Jimmy looked at her. 'Yes.'

She cupped his cheek with her hand and looked him straight in the eye. 'It's not like last time, even a little bit?' Aunt Min probed.

'No, honestly. Everyone's kind to me and I like it here. I miss you very much, Aunt Min, but if I've got to be away from you, then this is the best place to be.'

Aunt Min nodded. 'I had to be completely sure that you're safe.' She put her arm around Jimmy's shoulders. 'I'm glad you're well cared for and happy here. I was worried, but now I can see I had no need to be. It's a weight off my mind.'

Jimmy weaved his bike from side to side, loving the feeling of swooping and turning, being the closest he could get to flying while still on the ground. He laughed out loud, feeling nearly fit to burst with happiness because everything in his world was perfect; now Aunt Min was staying, he had all the people who he cared for together in the place he'd come to love. Life was good.

He was on his way back to the farm after delivering

the eggs to the shop because Aunt Min had insisted he keep up with his usual jobs on the farm while she was there. Ned and Jacob had also gone off delivering boxes of fruit and vegetables to the nearest station.

Jimmy would never have dared ride like this if he'd had a load of precious eggs in the front basket, because if he'd broken them Bea would be upset and disappointed in him. He'd hate that, so he'd ridden carefully on the way, and saved up the fun bit for on the way back, when his job was done and he was free to enjoy himself.

Admiring the view from high up on the saddle, Jimmy surveyed the surrounding fields where the corn had been cut and stood upright in stooks to dry. A sudden movement on the road ahead caught his attention and he turned in time to see someone run across the road and disappear into a field on the other side. That was odd.

Jimmy pedalled on until he was level with the field where the person had disappeared, and he stopped, putting his foot down on the bank to steady himself so he could stay sitting on the saddle, his high perch giving him a clear view over the hedge top. He could see a man standing a little way into the field peering down at something box-shaped in his hand. Jimmy couldn't be sure, but it looked like a camera. What had he been taking pictures of around here? Why was he cutting across roads and through fields? Why not go along the road like everyone else . . . unless of course it was because he didn't want to be seen? Who was he? A feeling of fear gripped Jimmy's stomach and his heartbeat quickened. Was he a German spy, parachuted in under cover of darkness to spy on the local bases, so he could tell Hitler's bombers where to come?

The man suddenly moved off, walking at a fast pace and hugging the hedgerow around the edge of the field. He was heading in the direction of Catchetts Farm. If he went there everyone on the farm could be in danger. The thought of something happening to any of them made Jimmy's insides lurch. He had to stop him.

A surge of adrenaline surged through Jimmy. He had to do something, and quick. Phylly would know what to do – she'd help him. Pushing off hard against the bank to give himself a good start, Jimmy pedalled fast, his heart pumping hard inside his chest. He wished that his bike could really fly, then he'd be able to go as the crow flies and not have to take the winding road back to the farm. The man would be there much quicker going cross-country. Who would get there first?

Jimmy's leg muscles were burning by the time he turned into the track leading down to Catchetts Farm. Glancing over the hedgetops, he spotted the man again – he'd reached Catchetts Farm land, and was moving along the far hedge of Five Acres field.

Putting on another burst of speed, Jimmy bumped and bounced his bike off stones as it jolted its way along the unpaved surface; he had to concentrate hard and hold on tight to stop himself being thrown off. At last he reached the farmyard and headed to where Phylly had been hoeing in the cabbage field earlier that morning. He rode straight into the field, pedalling hard until his bicycle ploughed to a halt in the soft earth. Phylly was still there, hoeing near the end of the row not far from the gate. Too breathless to shout, Jimmy gave a single ring of his bicycle bell to attract her attention.

Phylly looked up and came running over. 'Jimmy, are you all right?'

'A man . . . ' he gasped, drawing in a great lungful of air, 'coming this way. . . . spy . . . got to . . . stop . . . him.'

'Where?'

'Five Acres . . . nearly here . . . ' Jimmy looked over towards the gate where this field joined Five Acres, his stomach knotting in fear, because any moment the man could be there. 'Must . . . stop . . . him . . . '

Letting his bike fall to the ground, Jimmy started to run towards Five Acres. Phylly followed him, carrying her hoe with her. As they reached Gracie, who was working further across the field, Phylly grasped the other Land Girl's arm and ordered, 'Bring your hoe.'

'What's going on?' Gracie said.

'Just come!'

Reaching the gateway into the Five Acres, Phylly got hold of Jimmy.

'Wait.' She peered round the hedge and immediately pulled back. 'He's there under the tree,' she whispered. 'Looking at a camera or something.'

'Who is he?' Gracie whispered.

'A spy,' Jimmy kept his voice low. 'We've got to catch him.'

'How?' Gracie said. 'We should go for the police.'

'No time,' Phylly said. 'He's coming this way. Get on the other side of the gate, Gracie, hide.'

Phylly pulled Jimmy back to one side of the gate where they were hidden behind the hedge, and raised her hoe in the air, motioning for Gracie to do the same. Then they waited.

It felt like an age to Jimmy but it must have only been a matter of seconds before the man appeared and climbed over the gate into their field. The moment his feet touched the ground, Phylly roared '*Now!*' springing forward, bringing her hoe down in front of him, and Gracie followed suit, the two of them pinning him against the gate.

The spy looked stunned, then burst into rapid speech

in another language and waved his hands wildly in the air. Jimmy didn't understand a word of it, but one thing was for sure – he wasn't English.

'What are we going to do with him?' Gracie asked.

'We need to lock him in somewhere till help arrives,' Phylly said. 'Jimmy, can you go for the police, as quick as you can?'

Jimmy nodded and ran as fast as he could back to his bike and heaved it up from the ground. Putting his foot on the pedal, ready to scoot off, he glanced back to where Phylly and Gracie were marching the spy back towards the farm, his hands up above his head, and both Land Girls had their hoes poised ready to take action if he tried to make a run for it. Jimmy hoped he wouldn't – he'd seen how they tackled weeds, they'd have no problem in bringing him down between them, unless of course the spy had a gun . . . he'd have been trained to use it and was probably waiting for his chance. Jimmy hesitated. Should he risk leaving the Land Girls alone with the spy while he went for help?

'Go on Jimmy, what are you waiting for?' Phylly shouted. 'Hurry!'

There was nothing for it but to do as Phylly said. Hoping that he was doing the right thing, Jimmy pushed off with his foot, threw his leg over the crossbar and pedalled as fast as he could for the police house in the village.

Chapter Five

Jimmy paced up and down, stopping every few minutes to peer out of the kitchen window, looking for any sign, any clue which might tell him what was going on. Were the police arresting the spy? Were they interrogating him?

'What *are* they doing? Why don't they tell us what's going on?' Jimmy said, venting his frustration. The others waiting in the kitchen with him knew as much as he did, but they looked a lot calmer. Florrie, Bea, Aunt Min and the two Land Girls were all sitting around the kitchen table drinking tea.

'I'm sure they know what they're doing,' Florrie said, shooting a glance at Phylly, who shrugged hers shoulders in response. 'We've just got to be patient.'

Jimmy glanced at the clock on the wall, whose hands hardly seemed to have moved since last time he looked. When he'd come rushing back to the farm with the village policeman, both of them on their bikes, racing along till they were red in the face and puffing like trains, he'd never expected to be bundled away indoors out of the way to wait. He'd spotted the spy, raised the alarm, and had been prepared to stay there and do his part to the bitter end, but he didn't get the chance – the policeman had immediately taken over, ordering Jimmy and the Land Girls inside the house for their own safety, while he took over standing guard outside the shed in which the spy was locked until more reinforcements arrived.

It was out of Jimmy's hands and all he'd been able to do was watch as the farmyard had filled with more arrivals, first more policemen and then, just a few minutes ago, an army officer who'd been quickly ushered into the shed.

Had he come to start interrogating the spy? Jimmy

wondered. Perhaps he was trained in how to find out information and would know all the tricks a spy would use to talk his way out of trouble. Jimmy's imagination was busy weaving tales, coming up with ideas of what was going on, when there was a loud knock at the door, making him jump.

'I'll go.' Jimmy launched himself towards the door.

'No, Jimmy!' Aunt Min stood up and grabbed his arm as he went past her.

'I'll go,' Bea said.

Everyone watched in silence as Bea opened the door to reveal their village policeman smiling in at them.

'You can come out now,' he said. 'It's quite safe.'

When he walked out into the farmyard, Jimmy was shocked to see that the spy was out of the shed, standing there as bold as brass beside the army officer. He wasn't even handcuffed. He was free.

'I'm pleased to tell you that everything is quite in order,' the policeman said. 'Monsieur Maupin here is in fact a member of the Free French Forces and was finding his way back to his camp on a training exercise.

This,' the policeman held up what Jimmy had thought was a camera, 'is his compass, which he was using to navigate his way back.'

'So, he's not a spy then?' Florrie said.

'No, Mrs Bray, he's not.'

'He looked like one—' Jimmy began.

'Shhhh!' Aunt Min laid a hand on Jimmy's shoulder.

'It's all right, lad,' said the army officer. 'You did the right thing. Anyone looking suspicious should be reported, and you were brave doing what you did. A real spy could've had a gun.'

The spy, or Monsieur Maupin, as they should think of him, spoke to the army officer in rapid French.

The officer nodded and then translated it for them. 'Monsieur Maupin isn't upset about what happened – he says you were correct to do as you did, it was good practice for him. He will face worse things when he goes back to France.' He paused and smiled broadly. 'Perhaps we should incorporate avoiding boys and Land Girls armed with hoes into all our training exercises.'

*

Phylly was grateful for the cloudy, overcast day as it kept the temperature down in the greenhouse where she and Gracie were picking ripe tomatoes. They were working in silence as Gracie clearly wasn't in the mood for talking again. She'd been quieter than ever in the days since the-spy-who-wasn't incident.

At the sound of the door opening, Phylly turned to see who it was.

'Hello, Bea. It's not time for break yet, is it?' Phylly began, but stopped when she saw the worried look on Bea's face and what she was holding in her hand.

'The postman's just delivered this,' Bea held out a letter to Gracie. 'It looks official, it might be . . . '

Gracie took the letter and stared at it for a few moments, then tore it open, took out the letter and began to read.

Phylly's gaze met Bea's as they waited, an unspoken message passing between them. Would it be good news? Or bad?

Gracie must have been holding her breath, as she suddenly took in a great lungful of air and erupted into loud sobs. Phylly immediately put her arms around her friend, fearing the worst had happened.

'I'm so sorry, Gracie,' Phylly said.

Gracie shook her head. 'No, it's all right. He's . . . alive! Richard's alive! Look!'

Scanning rapidly through the words, Phylly read that Richard was now officially a prisoner of war, and it gave an address where Gracie could write to him.

'Thank goodness.' Phylly hugged Gracie tightly. 'That is such good news.'

'He's out of it now.' Gracie beamed. 'No more flying on dangerous missions.'

'I'm so happy for you,' Bea said. 'Now you'll be able to write to him and send him parcels.'

Gracie nodded, dashing tears away from her cheeks. 'I can knit him some socks and a scarf to send.'

'I thought you couldn't knit.' Phylly said.

'I can't,' Gracie smiled. 'But now I've got a good reason to learn.'

*

Phylly pushed the last pin into place and checked that the hem looked straight all the way around the bottom of her dress.

'Is it all right, Phylly?' Florrie asked from where she sat at the other end of the kitchen table beside Aunt Min, the two of them slicing their way through a pile of runner beans for dinner.

'It'll be fine once I've sewn it up.' Phylly gently eased the hem under the needle of Bea's sewing machine, then dropped the foot down on to the material.

'I'm glad you've got a chance to go dancing – you work hard and deserve some fun,' Florrie said.

'You've got to grab every chance you get these days,' Aunt Min said. 'You should see all the servicemen and women out enjoying themselves in London.'

'I've never been to London.' Phylly slowly turned the wheel on the sewing machine, which sent the needle bobbing up and down through the material of her dress. 'I'd like to go there one day.'

'Best wait till the rockets stop falling . . .' Florrie

stopped and bit her lip. 'Sorry, Min, you're living with that every day.'

'Don't worry, Florrie, it's a fact and we just have to get on with it. But you're right, it'd be best to wait till it's safer before you come to London, Phylly. That's why I had to send Jimmy here. I couldn't risk him being hurt after I promised his father I'd look after him.'

'You went through the Blitz together, didn't you?' Florrie asked.

'Yes, that was bad enough, but at least we got some warning. These doodlebugs are different.' Aunt Min shook her head. 'I had no choice but to risk evacuating Jimmy again and just hope it didn't turn out like last time . . . it's been such a worry.'

'Jimmy told us about it, poor lad,' Phylly said.

Aunt Min stopped slicing the bean she was working on and sighed heavily. 'The people he was billeted with didn't want him, they were only interested in getting the billeting allowance that came for keeping him.' Aunt Min paused, blinking rapidly behind her glasses.

'I was frantic with worry when he didn't write to me again after his first postcard telling me where he was, so I went to see him and found out what had been going on. Broke my heart to see how scared and lonely he was . . .' Her voice cracked and she sniffed hard, waiting a few moments to compose herself before she went on. 'I took Jimmy straight back home to London and I swore I'd never send him away again, but when the doodlebugs started . . .'

Florrie put her hand on Aunt Min's arm. 'You did the right thing. Jimmy's safe here and he's happy.'

Aunt Min nodded and smiled. 'Yes, he is. I can see how well you all look after and care for him, especially Bea.'

'She was born to be a mother,' Florrie said. 'Even when she was a little girl she'd mother things, a kitten or a younger child.' A shadow passed over Florrie's face. 'It's a terrible shame she's never got to mother her own children. There was a chance once, but she lost the baby before it was born . . . right after her husband died from the Spanish flu.'

'Poor Bea, I didn't know,' Phylly said. Bea had never spoken about her lost child; it must have hurt her badly.

'It's a pity she never remarried,' Aunt Min said.

Florrie sighed. 'I hoped she might one day, but she hasn't so far. So your Jimmy's getting all her maternal love poured into him instead.' She squeezed Aunt Min's arm. 'You've no fear that he's not being well cared for and loved.'

It would be a hard blow to Bea if Aunt Min *had* come to take him home, as she feared was going to happen, Phylly thought. Nobody had actually asked Aunt Min if that was why she'd come. Someone should though, for Bea's sake.

Phylly stopped the wheel of the sewing machine and looked at Aunt Min. 'Are you going to take Jimmy back to London with you?'

Aunt Min looked shocked. 'No, of course not! I came here so I could check Jimmy's *truly* as happy as he sounds in his letters. I had to be sure about that, you understand.' She smiled at Phylly and Florrie. 'But coming here and seeing how well you all look after him has satisfied me – all my worries have all gone and I want him to stay here with you until it's safe for him to come home. I miss him very much, but I'm *not* going to put him at risk. A bit of missing is a small price to pay for his safety.'

'We *were* worried that you'd come to take him home . . .' Florrie admitted. 'I'm glad you're happy that he's truly cared for here.' She took hold of Aunt Min's hand. 'You know, you could stay here, too, not go back to London until it's safe. We'd be glad to have you stay and Jimmy certainly would.'

Aunt Min nodded, squeezing Florrie's hand. 'I appreciate your offer, I really do, but I'm city born and bred. It's lovely out here in the countryside but I'm best at home in the city. I'll come back and visit from time to time, though, if that's all right.'

Gracie paused outside the greenhouse for a moment, feeling like she used to before she went into her old headmistress's office after a summoning for some misdemeanour or other – only her recent behaviour was far worse than playing some prank on one of her fellow pupils. The way she'd behaved was utterly shameful. Standing up to her full height, squaring her shoulders and with her chin up, Gracie opened the greenhouse door and stepped into the warmth to try to make amends.

Her arrival was immediately spotted by Benedict and Roberto, who were taking their turn at picking the ripe tomatoes, which was now a daily job on the farm. Both men nodded politely and returned to their work. Gracie swallowed hard against the solid lump of guilt which felt like it had wedged itself in her chest. It was written all over the POWs' faces how wary they were of her. They were never like that with Phylly, always greeting her with warmth and delight, but then she'd welcomed them from the start and only shown them friendship and help, whereas Gracie . . . she'd been cold and unwelcoming, shunning them as if they were responsible for this horrid war. But it wasn't their doing, they'd been caught up in it because they were made to and not because they wanted to. They were glad to be out of it now, and since coming to work at the farm, they had proven themselves over and over again with their hard work, good nature and kindness to everyone. That made her behaviour towards them even more unforgivable. Would they forgive her . . . or at least give her a chance?

'Benedict, Roberto,' Gracie said, stepping towards them.

They both stopped picking and looked at her.

'I . . . I want to tell you both how very sorry I am for the way I've treated you. It was utterly wrong and I'm ashamed of myself, I . . . '

Benedict held out his hand to her as she faltered. 'Is fine, Gracie, we no angry.'

She took hold of his hand and smiled at him as they shook hands. 'Thank you.'

Then Benedict turned and spoke to Roberto in rapid Italian, explaining what Gracie had told him, the two of them having a brief conversation.

'Roberto say he always think it because you so sad, see it in your eyes.'

Gracie swallowed hard and nodded, holding out her hand to Roberto who shook it, smiling warmly at her.

'It's no excuse, but I was so worried, so horribly worried about my husband flying on his missions. I felt like I was living on a knife edge, never knowing if he was coming back . . . and I took it out on you . . .' Her voice wavered and she paused for a moment to compose herself. 'When he went missing . . .'

'Phylly told us what happened,' Benedict said. 'She very worried about you.'

Gracie nodded, blinking back the tears. 'But then I found out that Richard is now a prisoner of war . . . he's like you . . . and I understood.'

Benedict took hold of her hands in both of his. 'We glad he safe now, no more fighting, he just wait till the war over and come home to you.'

'Yes,' Gracie's voice came out in a squeak. 'Still, I am ashamed of how I behaved towards you. Do you think you could forgive me and perhaps even become friends?'

'We like very much to be your friend,' Benedict said, beaming at her, his blue eyes twinkling brightly in his tanned face.

'There, how's that?' Gracie smiled at Phylly in the mirror. 'That should hold even if you are dancing all night.'

Phylly looked at her reflection in the mirror, turning her head first to one side and then the other to see what Gracie had done with her hair. She'd brushed it out and pinned it to make the most of her natural wave and it looked good, much smarter than it usually did. 'Thank you,' she said. 'It looks lovely.'

'Good. Now we just need to do your make-up and you're ready.' Gracie put her hands on Phylly's shoulders and turned her around in the chair until she was facing her.

'Are you sure you don't want to come? It'll be fun to go dancing.' Phylly asked.

'Yes, I'm quite sure, but I'm glad that you're going.' Gracie took the lid off Phylly's lipstick which Edwin's mother had sent from America. 'Hush now, while I put this on – lips wide like this, please.' She pulled her own lips into a wide oval shape to demonstrate.

Phylly did as she was told and kept silent while Gracie applied the lipstick and then some powder.

'There – you don't need make-up to look beautiful, Phylly, you already are,' Gracie said, finishing dusting her nose with the powder puff. 'Just as well we don't have much of it.' She smiled, putting her hand on Phylly's shoulder. 'Have a lovely time tonight with the delightful Edwin. He adores you, you know, you only have to see the way he looks at you.'

Phylly felt her cheeks grow warm. 'Edwin likes everyone, he's a friendly person.'

'He is, but he only has eyes for you!' Gracie laughed. 'Just enjoy yourself tonight, you deserve some fun. You work so hard.'

'So do you. There's still time for you to put on a frock and do your hair,' Phylly encouraged her.

'No, I'm going to write to my darling Richard. You can tell me all about it when you get home. I'll want to hear every detail about the band and the dances, everything.'

Phylly laughed. 'Very well, I'll report back later on.'

'Good, I'll wait up for you.'

As the last notes died away and the band left the small stage to take a break, Phylly realised how thirsty she was. Since she and Edwin had arrived at the Hundreth Mission, they had done nothing but dance, caught up in the addictive toe-tapping music. Together they had twirled and whirled around, enjoying the music and the happy atmosphere that filled the huge hangar, which had been beautifully decorated and turned into a dance hall for the evening.

'Can I get you a drink?' Edwin asked.

Phylly nodded. 'I'd love one, thank you. It's thirsty work, this dancing, but I'm loving it.'

Edwin smiled. 'Me, too. I'm glad you could come, Phylly.'

They made their way over to where the refreshments were being served and joined the queue for drinks.

'Edwin! Is this the famous Phylly?'

The mention of her name made Phylly turn around to see another American standing behind her in the queue.

'Phylly, meet Joe, he's a member of our crew,' Edwin said.

'Glad to meet you, Phylly,' Joe held out his hand. 'We've heard lots about you.'

Phylly shook his hand. 'All good, I hope?'

'Oh yes; in fact—' Joe began.

'It's our turn,' Edwin interrupted. 'Lemonade or tea, Phylly?'

'Lemonade, please,' Phylly said. 'What were you about to say, Joe?'

'That you're Edwin's favourite topic of conversation, you know he—'

'If you'll excuse us, Joe,' Edwin handed Phylly a glass of cool lemonade and took hold of her elbow. 'We're gonna go outside and get some fresh air before the dancing starts again.'

'But . . . ' Phylly looked back at Joe, who grinned at

her and waved as Edwin steered her away. 'What was that about?' she asked as Edwin led her out through the huge hangar doors into the cooler evening air. 'Why did you cut him off like that?'

'Joe's got a way of letting his mouth run away with itself. He . . . '

'He what?'

Edwin took a sip of his lemonade and looked uncomfortable.

'Edwin? What's the matter?'

'Let's go and sit over there, where it's quieter.' He took hold of her elbow again and led her away from where more and more people were spilling out of the hangar to enjoy the cool air.

'I'm listening,' Phylly said, once they were sitting down on the grass a little way off from the hangar.

Edwin took a deep breath and looked at her, his blue eyes holding hers. 'You mean a lot to me, Phylly. I love being with you and when I'm not, then I'm thinking about you . . . or talking about you to the others, like Joe.'

'You didn't want Joe to give the game away?'

Edwin nodded. 'I've been plucking up the courage to tell you how I feel about you. Will you be my girl, Phylly?'

She stared at him for a few moments and then took a sip of her lemonade to delay answering, glad of its sharp, refreshing taste as it gave her senses a sharp tug and kept her grounded.

Edwin took hold of her hand. 'What do you think?' His eyes were full of hope.

Phylly squeezed his hand gently. 'You are the loveliest, kindest man . . . ' she smiled at him. 'I love being with you too, and if . . . ' She paused, taking in a deep breath to keep herself steady, to keep her voice from betraying the turmoil that was boiling up inside her, as what she felt in her heart battled it out with what she'd learned in her head. 'If this war was over, then we'd be free to . . . but I can't, not yet . . . ' Phylly's eyes filled with tears. 'It's not that I don't want to . . . '

'If you really want to, what's stopping you?'

Phylly sighed. 'Remember I told you about my

fiancé getting killed at Dunkirk . . . I don't want to go through that again, the worry, not knowing and then finding out he'd—' She shook her head. 'No one knows what's going to happen, even if any of us will be here tomorrow with this war on.'

'I know that.' Edwin frowned. 'Don't you think we always wonder if we'll come back from a mission? That's why we should seize the chance now, while we can.'

'I'm sorry, Edwin, I just can't. There's too much of a risk to let myself really care for you and then if . . .' Tears spilled over and ran down her face. 'It's not because I don't want to . . . I do . . . I'm just too scared.' She wiped her tears away with the back of her hand.

Edwin nodded. 'I'm sorry too, but I understand your reasons.' He looked thoughtful. 'How about if I finish my missions and then volunteer for a ground job so I could stay here instead of going back to the States with the rest of the crew? Will you be my girl then?'

Phylly nodded and smiled at him.

He put his arm around her shoulders. 'OK, if I can't

persuade you to change your mind, then I can wait – you're worth waiting for, Phylly.'

'Thank you.' She leaned against him, wishing with both her heart and her head that the war would end and it would be safe to love again, and most of all hoping that she had made the right decision.

Jimmy clung tightly on to Aunt Min's hand as they stood waiting at the bus stop by the village green on Monday morning. He and Bea had come to see Aunt Min off, and now the precious seconds left with her were ebbing away fast. He desperately hoped that the bus wouldn't turn up so it couldn't take her away to the nearest station to get the train to Norwich, then she wouldn't be able to change to the London train to take her home. He didn't want her to go.

Looking up at her, Jimmy decided to try again, ask her the same question he'd put to her several times over the weekend. 'Why don't you stay, Aunt Min? Please.'

Not waiting for an answer, he threw himself against her and wrapped his arms around her. She responded, enfolding him in her own arms, making Jimmy want to stay like that for ever, but after a few, too-short moments, Aunt Min loosened her arms and took a step back so she could look him straight in the eye.

'Now, Jimmy, we've already talked about why I can't stay. I need to go back home to London because staying here in the country wouldn't be right for me, but I promise you, I'll come back again soon.'

'Florrie said you could live with us until London's safe again.'

'I know she did, and it's very kind of her, but it just wouldn't be right for *me.* The important thing is that you're happy here, and that makes me happy, too.' She squeezed his shoulder. 'You're safe here.'

'But I miss you.' Jimmy's throat was hurting and his eyes smarted with tears, making Aunt Min's face look all blurry.

'I miss you, too. Remember we're not the only ones – there are lots of people missing each other in wartime. When it's all over we'll be back together again.' Aunt Min smiled.

'The bus's coming,' Bea said, nodding towards the bus, which was coming along the road towards them and would be at the stop in a matter of seconds.

Aunt Min nodded and held out her hand to shake Bea's. 'Thank you very much for all your kindness and for taking such good care of Jimmy. I'm glad he's in your safe hands.'

'It's been a pleasure to get to know you.' Bea shook Aunt Min's hand. 'And if you do change your mind, the offer to come and stay at Catchetts is always open.'

'Thank you, I really do appreciate that. Now, Jimmy,' Aunt Min paused as the bus drew up alongside them and passengers began to get off. 'Will you keep writing your lovely letters to me, telling me what you've been up to?'

Jimmy nodded, unable to speak – his throat felt as if it was been squeezed tight with sadness.

'I'll be back to see you again soon.' Aunt Min bent down and kissed him on his cheek. 'I'm always with you in spirit,' she whispered in his ear. 'Always remember that.'

Jimmy flung his arms around her and hugged her tightly, shutting his eyes and hoping that by some miracle Aunt Min would change her mind at this last moment and stay.

'Jimmy.' Bea touched his shoulder. 'It's time for Aunt Min to get on the bus now.'

The miracle he hoped for wasn't going to happen. Jimmy gave Aunt Min one last squeeze and let her go. 'Goodbye.' His voice sounded rough.

'Goodbye, Jimmy.' Aunt Min squeezed his shoulder and then climbed up into the bus, carrying her case and a basket packed with extras from the farm – some of Florrie's butter, eggs, fruit and vegetables, which would help improve her meagre rations for a while.

Bea put her arm around Jimmy's shoulders as they watched Aunt Min through the bus windows. She settled down in a seat next to a window and smiled out at them. Jimmy did his best to smile back, but it was hard when inside he felt like crying, so he waved at Aunt Min, who waved back at him. They kept on waving to each other as the bus pulled away, Aunt Min turning around in her seat to look back until the bus rounded the corner and vanished from sight.

Jimmy stopped waving and let his hand fall limply to his side. He couldn't hold back his tears any longer, and they slid hotly down his cheeks.

'Why couldn't she stay, Bea?' he said, the pain in his throat making it hard to talk.

'I think she needs to be where she feels at home, and that's in London. When you're older it's hard to change things. She'll be back to see you again soon.'

Jimmy sniffed. 'I want to be with her there and be here too.'

'I know.' Bea put both her arms around him and held him tightly. 'It's hard for you to be apart, but it's important to Aunt Min that you're safe from the doodlebugs for now. You'll be starting school here next week, so you'll soon be busy with that. Aunt Min will want to know about it in your letters.'

School! The thought of starting at a new school didn't do anything to cheer Jimmy up. Right now, he felt completely miserable – Aunt Min was on her way back to London, and Bea had just reminded him that from next week, he'd have to spend days sitting still doing sums and learning spellings. There'd be no more summer days out working on the farm with the Land Girls or POWs or chasing spies-who-weren't. The thought of those happy days of summer coming to an end just made Jimmy feel worse.

Jimmy scuffed his shoes hard against the dry soil, sending puffs of dust spiralling upwards into the air where it was caught by the breeze and sent tumbling and scattering across the yard. He kicked again, watching as more dust danced higher into the air.

'Mind my clean washing!' Florrie's voice made Jimmy jump.

He turned to see her watching him, hand on one hip, the other balancing the empty wicker washing basket against her side. Behind her, around the other side of the farmhouse in the side garden, and luckily in the opposite direction to where the kicked-up dust had blown, were several lines of clean sheets flapping and snapping in the breeze.

'If you keep kicking that dust about and it gets on my clean sheets, then you and I are going to fall out,' Florrie added. 'Bea and I have got enough to do this morning without having to rewash sheets.'

'I'm sorry,' Jimmy said, his face growing hot.

Florrie smiled at him. 'Go on then, get them drinks and snacks delivered and then you can come back and help me. Take your frustration out on the mangle. Cranking that handle round and round is good for when you're feeling out of sorts.'

Jimmy nodded and picked up the basket that Bea had given him to take round to the Land Girls and POWs and hurried off to where they were working in the greenhouse. He didn't mean to upset Florrie – he hadn't thought, just kicked. He'd never intentionally mess up the sheets and it was lucky for him that the wind had been blowing in the other direction. It was this mood he was in, it had settled on him on the way back from the village and hovered over him like a black cloud. He'd so desperately wanted Aunt Min to stay but she hadn't and there wasn't a thing he could do to change it – and that hurt.

Bea had tried to cheer him up and he knew why she'd sent him out with the basket – it was to keep him busy, take his mind off things. Only it hadn't worked. Maybe cranking the mangle might help, he'd give it a try after he'd delivered the basket.

Walking into the greenhouse, Jimmy was surprised to see that everyone had already stopped work. They were gathered around Roberto, who was sitting on an upturned wooden crate with one leg stretched out in front of him, Phylly knelt beside him examining his ankle.

'Ah, Jimmy,' Benedict called to him.

'What's happened? What's wrong with Roberto?'

'He's hurt his ankle,' Phylly said. 'I don't think it's broken, it's probably a sprain, but the camp doctor needs to have a look at it to be sure.'

'No fuss,' Benedict said. 'Roberto he no want fuss.'

'But you're hurt,' Jimmy said kneeling down beside Roberto.

'Been hurt, more like it,' Gracie said crossly, her hands on her hips. 'It was that guard, the mean-faced one, he was in a really nasty mood this morning from the look of him, and when Roberto didn't get out of the truck quick enough to suit him, he yanked him out so he landed badly and twisted his ankle. I saw it all out of the kitchen window.'

'Then he should be punished for hurting Roberto,' Jimmy said. 'It's not right.'

'No, it isn't,' Gracie said. 'Prisoners of war have rights and should be treated well, there's the Geneva Convention. We have to do something . . . '

Benedict shook his head, holding out his hands. 'We no want fuss, is fine, Roberto is fine in day or two.'

'That guard is horrible!' Jimmy burst out.

'*Si*, he not nice, today he in hurry to go—' Benedict stopped and looked down at his boots.

'Go where?' Phylly asked.

Benedict shrugged and turned to Jimmy. 'Some tea?'

Jimmy looked at Phylly who nodded at him to do as Benedict asked, so he took the bottles of cold tea out of the basket and passed them around to everyone, feeling like he wanted to know more, ask more about what going on. What had Benedict been about to say? Where was the guard going in a hurry? Wherever it was, his job was to look after the POWs first, make sure they were taken to their farms safely, not yanked out of an army truck so they hurt themselves.

Jimmy had a bad feeling about this. He'd never liked the guard from the first time he saw him – he was like a dog that wanted to bite you. Now there was something funny going on and his friends were getting hurt. There was nothing he could do about the problem of Aunt Min going, but perhaps there was something he could do about this.

As the two POWs drank their cold tea, Jimmy vowed to himself that he would find out what was going on. He'd be watching and waiting and would do anything he could to protect his friends.

Chapter Six

Jimmy watched as the army truck drove into the farm-yard, swung around in a wide arc and came to a halt with a jerking of its brakes. From his look-out post, high up under the eaves of the farmhouse, tucked well out of sight behind his bedroom curtains, Jimmy could see everything that went on. If something else happened to the POWs then he would witness it for himself.

The passenger door of the cab flew open and the mean guard jumped out and hurried around to the back of the truck, banging hard on the side as he went.

'Let's be 'avin yar!' he bellowed.

From his lofty viewpoint, Jimmy could see that Benedict and Roberto were already standing at the end of the truck waiting for the guard to drop down the tail gate to let them out. They weren't going to give him the slightest reason to hurt them again, not after he'd yanked Roberto out of the truck two weeks ago and hurt his ankle. Since then Jimmy had been watching the Italians arrive and leave every day, just in case anything else happened, but it hadn't. Not yet.

The guard dropped the tail gate and the moment the POWs' boots hit the dusty ground he started raising it again, quickly securing it in place, before running back and climbing in the cab, slamming the door with a loud thud as the driver put the lorry into gear and drove away far too fast, leaving behind a cloud of exhaust fumes.

They were in a hurry again, Jimmy thought. Where were they going in such a hurry? Benedict and Roberto were always the last POWs to be dropped off, so it wasn't because they needed to get to another farm. Perhaps he shouldn't worry about it – as long as Benedict and Roberto were safe and unharmed, that was the important thing. Now they'd arrived at Catchetts Farm, Jimmy could rest easy as he knew they'd be safe here for the day, at least until it was time for them to be collected later in the afternoon, and then he'd be back at his look-out post to watch them being picked up.

In the meantime, the rest of Jimmy's day was sadly accounted for – he had to go to school. That had started last week and was the part of his life that he didn't like very much, but which he knew had to be tolerated. His new school in the village was very different from his big London school; this one had just two classes, one for the infants and one for the juniors, but there were still spellings to learn, long division sums to do . . .

'Jimmy?' Bea called up the stairs. 'You need to get going or you'll be late for school.'

Jimmy sighed. 'Coming.'

Reaching up on tiptoe, Jimmy plucked the large blackberry which was dangling temptingly at the centre of a large cluster of berries that were still red and hadn't yet ripened to a glossy black colour. Popping it into his mouth, he chewed slowly, releasing the mellow, fruity taste which he'd come to love. He'd never tried blackberries before he'd come to live at Catchetts Farm, but since Bea had introduced him to them on one of her many blackberrying expeditions, he'd more than made up for it by eating them whenever he could, and this morning they were a welcome distraction as he dawdled his way to school.

As he reached out for another, being careful to not disturb a spider who was sitting motionless in the middle of its intricate web, Jimmy heard the sound of an engine coming towards him along the narrow lane. There wasn't much room to pass, so he quickly slipped into a nearby gateway to wait until it had gone. Jimmy nearly choked on the blackberry he was chewing when the vehicle rounded the corner and he saw who it was – the same army truck that had brought Benedict and Roberto to the farm earlier, with the same mean guard and driver on board. They flashed by quickly, too quickly for them to have seen him in his spot tucked away in the gateway, and for some strange reason, Jimmy felt relieved. He didn't want to meet them away from the safety of the farm.

But where had they been? he wondered. They hadn't come from the direction of the POW camp, that was way off on the other side of the nearest town, and they couldn't have been delivering any other Italians to farms, as Benedict and Roberto were always the last to be dropped off.

Stepping back onto the road, Jimmy noticed faint, dark tyre prints on the grey surface which had been left by the truck. He squatted down to examine them, prodding them with his finger to find they were slightly damp. Strange, because it hadn't been raining and there were no puddles on the road. He stood up and like a hound on the scent, started to follow the prints back in the direction the truck had come from.

They led him back down the road a short way until they swung sharply to the left, off the road and straight into a large puddle which spanned the width of a dirt track.

Skirting around the edge of the puddle, taking care to avoid some tall nettles, Jimmy knelt down to look at the tyre tracks on the other side, where tell-tale splashes of muddy water coloured the soft, dry soil on the other side. There were definite tyre marks pressed into the soil which he could see led further off down the track away from the road. There was no doubt that the truck had been down the track. Standing up, Jimmy gazed at the tyre marks, trying to puzzle out why they had gone down there, because it didn't lead to a farm, only a wood. Why would the truck have gone down there? An uneasy feeling prickled along Jimmy's neck. There was something odd going on. What reason would the mean guard and the driver have to go up there? He had to find out.

He started to run along the track and then stopped after a few yards as his conscience prodded him – what about school? By now the teacher had probably come out and lined everyone up to go in. Even if he went straight there he'd be late and in trouble . . . and he desperately wanted to see if he could find out why the guards had gone up the track. Jimmy wavered for a few seconds and then he ran, but not in the direction of the school – he'd face any punishment for skipping school later. Right now, investigating this was much more important to him than practising long division sums.

Reaching the end of the track beside the wood, Jimmy could see where the truck had turned around, as there were tyre marks and crushed vegetation where the wheels had run off the edge of the track. Crouching low, he scouted around for more clues – and found footprints, large ones with the heavy tread pattern of army boots. Feeling like a detective, Jimmy followed the prints as they led him into the wood. Sometimes he lost the trail and had to search around until he picked it up again and gradually it led him to an old gamekeeper's hut tucked away in the wood, well out of sight of the track.

Why did they come here? What was going on? With his heart hammering hard, Jimmy tried the door – it was locked. He needed to look inside, but there weren't any windows. Skirting around the outside of the hut he searched for any hole or crack to spy through, but there weren't any. He was stumped – so close, but unable to get an answer. Jimmy kicked hard at a piece of fallen wood, sending it bouncing away across the floor of the wood until it disappeared from sight into the jungle of bracken. He was sure something was going on in there – those guards were up to something, probably something they shouldn't be doing. Why else would they come here? He needed help.

Should he go to the village constable again? But after the spy-who-wasn't-really incident the policeman might not believe him. No, there was only one person he could ask for help, and who wouldn't laugh at him – Phylly. She'd know what to do.

Keeping her weight carefully balanced against the ladder, Phylly reached across and picked a plump, purple plum, and gently put it in the basket strapped over her shoulders. There was a good crop this year and it was a rush to get them harvested before they lost too many to hungry wasps.

'Phylly!'

Hearing her name, she looked around to see who was calling her, but it was impossible to see through the mosaic of green leaves and purple plums. She knew it wasn't Gracie as she'd just gone back to the farmhouse with a basket of plums for Florrie, who wanted them to make into some jam to take with her when she went to visit her sister tomorrow. Gracie couldn't have got from the orchard and back so quickly.

'Phylly!' the voice came again.

'Who's there?'

'It's me! Jimmy!'

'Jimmy?' Phylly started to climb down the ladder, peering through the lower branches as she went, but she couldn't see him. 'Where are you?'

'Over here! Behind the hedge.'

Stepping off the ladder, Phylly shrugged off her basket of plums and hurried over to the hedge. 'Shouldn't you be at school?'

Jimmy's head suddenly popped up so she could see him through a thinner bit of hedge. 'Yes, that's why I'm hiding. If Bea or Florrie saw me . . .'

'What's going on, why aren't you there?'

'I need your help, Phylly.'

'How?'

As Jimmy explained what he'd found, Phylly felt a sense of unease well up inside her.

'So we need to find out what's in that shed,' Jimmy ended.

'It might be nothing, you know that,' Phylly said, keeping her voice calm. 'But on the other hand . . . that guard is a bad one, and Benedict's hinted at something . . .' She paused, thinking for a moment. 'We need to be sure. Wait here, Jimmy, I'll be back as quick as I can. Keep hidden.'

When she'd joined the Land Army, Phylly never imagined she'd be doing anything like this: running cross country, back the way that Jimmy had come from the wood, with a hammer and pliers in her hands, ready to do a bit of possible breaking and entering. She was sure it wasn't something that the Land Army organisers would approve of, but she couldn't just ignore what Jimmy had seen because her instinct told her that something odd was going on. She'd seen enough of the mean guard to know he was a bad sort and likely to be up to no good, but exactly what, she had no idea.

'What will we do if we find something?' Jimmy said running beside her.

'It depends *what* we find, *if* we find something.'

'What if's it's something bad?'

Phylly reached out her hand and grabbed Jimmy's arm to bring him to a halt beside her. 'We don't know what we're getting into here, but if it is something bad, then we'll need to go to the police. We can't deal with it ourselves, you need to understand that. Right, Jimmy?'

He nodded.

'The mean guard isn't the sort to mess around with, he's a nasty piece of work.' Phylly sighed. 'Let's just hope he doesn't come back while we're there.'

Jimmy's face turned pale. 'You don't think he will, do you?'

Phylly shrugged. 'I don't know, we need to be careful and not take any risks.'

'We'll be able to see if they've come back in the truck from quite a distance.'

'Good.' Phylly smiled at Jimmy. 'Come on, let's go and investigate.'

Phylly's insides felt like they were squirming around inside her as they approached the old gamekeeper's shed. She wasn't used to doing this sort of thing and part of her was frightened of what they might find. The main worry was that the guards would be there, and she'd been relieved to see that the army truck wasn't parked on the track and once they'd entered the wood, everywhere was quiet except for the rustlings of small animals and the sound of birds in the trees overhead.

'Are you going to break open the door?' Jimmy whispered.

'No, we can't do that as they'd know someone had been here. We need to look for a loose board and prise it open just enough to look inside. You look on that side and I'll look on this.' Phylly wanted to get this over as quickly as possible because there was always the danger that the guards might come back and catch them.

Feeling around the boards with her fingers they all seemed tight and secure. What they'd do if they couldn't find one, she wasn't sure. Phylly had almost searched all her side with no luck, when Jimmy called out.

'Found one!'

'Shhh!!' Phylly rushed around to find Jimmy kneeling down on the ground, his fingers wedged in between two boards, which he was wobbling to try to loosen even more. 'We're not supposed to be here, remember. Keep the noise down.'

'Sorry,' Jimmy whispered. 'Look, this board's loose here, you could lever it down further with the hammer then we can look in.'

Kneeling down beside Jimmy, Phylly put the claw end of the hammer between the boards started to lever them apart.

'Just a bit more,' Jimmy said.

Phylly pressed harder and there was a sharp crack, making them both jump, as the two boards prised apart.

'Quick, look inside while I hold them apart,' Phylly said.

Jimmy bent down and peered inside. 'I can't see much, there's a green thing blocking the way.'

'Let me see. Here, you hold the hammer for me.'

Jimmy took over holding the hammer while Phylly knelt down on all fours and looked in. 'It looks like a metal container.' She grabbed a nearby fallen stick, poked it through the hole and tapped it against the container, which made a tell-tale metal sound. 'It's definitely metal, and full of something by the sound of it . . . ' Phylly paused, her mind rushing ahead as an idea of what was inside the metal container formed in her mind. 'Pull the board down a bit more for me, Jimmy, I want to see a bit more.'

With the board pulled down as far as it would go, Phylly could see there were more of the metal containers lined up against the side of the shed. There could be even more, further in, but as far as she could see there were at least four of them and she knew exactly where she'd seen some like them before.

'Put the board back in place, Jimmy, we need to go to the police,' Phylly said, standing up and brushing the leaf mould off the knees of her brown Land Army dungarees.

'Why? What's in there?' Jimmy asked, handing her back the hammer.

'I think they're jerry cans and could be full of petrol.'

'Jerry cans! But why would the guards have them in here?'

'Petrol's rationed, so they could be selling it on the black market,' Phylly said. 'If it *is* what they're doing, then where did the petrol come from?'

'Do you think they stole it?'

Phylly shrugged. 'Possibly.' She put her arm around Jimmy's shoulders. 'We can't deal with this, Jimmy, it's far too serious.'

'So, you're telling me that there are cans of petrol in an old gamekeeper's hut in the middle of a wood?' the village constable asked, looking at Phylly and Jimmy with his shrewd brown eyes. 'This isn't another spy story, is it?'

'Of course not,' Phylly said. 'I can't be completely sure the cans are full of petrol, but they look like all the jerry cans I've ever seen before, they sound like they're full, and don't you think it's rather suspicious that they're stored in a hut in the middle of a wood, and visited by army guards who wouldn't normally be there?'

'Indeed, but I'd like to have a look for myself first before I take this any further, because if it is what you say it is, then I'm going to need help and a lot of it.'

'We can help you,' Jimmy said.

'The best thing you can do, son, is show me what you've found and if it is what you think, then it's going to be far too dangerous for you to be involved in. It'll be a job for the police and the Home Guard.'

'You mean Ned and Jacob?' Jimmy asked.

'Yes,' the constable said putting on his helmet. 'Off we go then, lead the way.'

'Phylly, where have you been?' Gracie leapt up from the kitchen table where the whole family were sitting drinking cups of tea. 'You just disappeared, we've been looking for you all over.'

'I'm sorry, but . . . ' Phylly began, as Jimmy and the constable walked into the kitchen behind her.

'Jimmy!' Bea jumped up from her chair and rushed over to him, her eyes checking him over to see if he was hurt. 'Why aren't you at school? What's going on?'

'Jimmy's been a clever lad and might have found some wrongdoings,' the constable explained. 'Ned, Jacob, I need the Home Guard's help, if we can talk in private . . . '

Ned nodded and stood up, 'We'll go in the front parlour.'

'What's it about?' Florrie said.

'No time to explain now, Mrs Bray, we need to mobilise the platoon,' the constable said. 'There'll be plenty of time to explain later.'

Jimmy stabbed his spoon into his porridge the next morning, trying to summon up an appetite for breakfast but failing miserably, because there was still no news.

Ned and Jacob had been out all night and hadn't come home yet. What was going on?

'I'll have to get word to my sister, tell her I can't come today after all,' Florrie said to Bea, as they both sat at the end of the kitchen table nursing cups of tea in their hands.

'She'll be disappointed,' Bea said.

'I know, but I can't go off gallivanting when I don't know what's happened and if Jacob and Ned are safe.' Florrie sighed. 'We don't even know where they are or what they're doing.'

Jimmy wished he could tell Florrie where they'd gone. She looked so worried, with dark circles under her eyes because in lieu of going to bed, she'd just sat dozing in the chair by the fire all night waiting for her husband and son to come home. But he couldn't tell her anything, because he'd promised the constable he wouldn't and Phylly had done the same.

'Do you want some more honey on your porridge?' Bea asked. 'Might help it go down a bit easier this morning.'

Jimmy shook his head. 'No, thank you. I'm not really hungry.'

'Eat it up, waste not want not,' Florrie said. 'Otherwise you'll be hungry all morning and won't be able to concentrate at school.'

'I can't go to school.' Tears smarted in Jimmy's eyes. 'Not until I know what's happened.'

Bea reached over and put a hand on his shoulder. 'You didn't go yesterday, Jimmy, so you must go today, Aunt Min wouldn't want you to miss out on your education.'

'I won't be able to concentrate with worrying about Jacob and Ned.'

'It'll help keep your mind off it.' Bea said. 'I need to go to the shop, so I'll walk down to the school with you to keep you company on the way.'

'Best to keep busy, Jimmy,' Florrie said, 'So eat up.'

Jimmy knew when he was beaten, so he scooped up a spoonful of honey-sweetened porridge and popped it into his mouth. But it didn't taste right, more like sawdust than the sweet deliciousness he usually loved.

*

Jimmy didn't feel like picking blackberries this morning. Walking to school beside Bea he held on to her hand, her warm fingers giving him gentle reassurance.

'Do you think they'll be back by the time I get home from school?' Jimmy asked.

'I've no idea. You know more about what might be happening than I do.'

Jimmy sighed. 'I hate not knowing what's going on. At least when we had the spy-who-wasn't incident we could look out of the window for clues. This time's much worse.'

'Try not to worry.' Bea squeezed his hand. 'Ned and my father know what they're doing – the Home Guard are trained to deal with all sorts of problems.'

Even hidden cans of petrol in a shed and mean army guards armed with rifles? Jimmy wondered. He shuddered at the thought of anything bad happening to Jacob or Ned; they'd both been so welcoming and kind to him since he'd come to live there and he'd grown to care for them. All he could do was be patient and wait for news, but it was hard.

For the rest of the walk into the village, Bea kept up a constant chatter, trying to take his mind off their worries, talking about things they saw, like the stoat that darted across the road in front of them, and some skylarks singing their sweet songs as they hovered above the meadow. Jimmy appreciated what she was doing, and normally he'd have been pleased to look at all those things with her, but this morning there was only one thing on his mind and it wasn't going to go anywhere until he had some answers.

He was so deep in thought about it that he didn't notice what was going on at first. As they neared the crossroads leading into the village he didn't realise who was standing there until Bea started running, and with his hand still clasped in hers, he was suddenly yanked along behind her. The movement brought him to the here and now and he sped up when he saw who they were running to – Ned and Jacob were standing talking to the constable.

'Dad! Ned!' Bea said, breathlessly from their quick sprint. 'Are you all right?'

'We're fine,' Jacob said, smiling at her. 'A good breakfast and a nap and we'll be as right as rain.'

'What happened?' Jimmy looking at them both for clues. They looked normal apart from a bit dirty and tired. 'Did the guards come back?'

'They did,' the constable said. 'And we were waiting for them. The Home Guard platoon had the area under surveillance and we caught them red-handed.' He started to chuckle. 'Or I should say red petrol-handed.'

'So, it was petrol in the cans?' Jimmy said.

'What's petrol got to do with it?' Bea asked.

The constable explained to her about Jimmy's discovery in the gamekeeper's hut. 'Phylly was right, they were full jerry cans. The guards had been stealing red army petrol and had set up a filtering system in the shed to get the red dye out. They were pouring it through a loaf of bread, would you believe, but it worked, took the dye out enough for them to sell the petrol on the black market.'

'Did you arrest them?' Jimmy asked.

'Of course. They won't be stealing anything again for a long time,' the constable said.

'They're a pair of fools,' Ned said. 'They were having an easy war compared with a lot of soldiers. They should've been happy with that but they got greedy and wanted to make some money.'

'They won't be making any more where they're going,' the constable said. He looked down at Jimmy. 'You did well, son. It had been going on for a while and no one knew about it until you found it. Well done, Jimmy – you'd make a fine detective. Thank you, Ned and Jacob, for your help; I couldn't have done it without you and the platoon. Right, I'm off for my breakfast.' He smiled at them and then headed off in the direction of the police house.

'What happened? How did you catch them?' Jimmy asked.

'You can find out about that later,' Bea said. 'You've got to go to school and Ned and Dad need their breakfasts. Mum's waiting for you and no doubt she'll cook you up a feast.'

'I thought she was going to see her sister today,' Jacob said.

'She's cancelled it, said she wasn't going anywhere till she knew you were home safe,' Bea said.

'We soon will be, so there's still time for her to go. Florrie's been looking forward to going to see her for weeks, she mustn't let this spoil it,' Jacob said. 'Come on, Ned, we'd better get home, so your mother can leave.'

'I'll be back soon, too,' Bea said. 'I'm going to go and explain why Jimmy wasn't at school yesterday and then go to the shop.' She put her arm around Jimmy's shoulders and started to steer him in the direction of the school. 'I'll see you back at the farm in a while.'

When Jimmy looked back over his shoulder, he saw that Ned and Jacob were already hurrying off in the direction of Catchetts Farm. He was desperate to know what had happened – he had so many questions to ask them – but it would have to wait until after school.

'That was delicious, Phylly. Thank you,' Jacob said, putting his knife and fork down on his empty plate and leaning back in his chair. 'Just the thing after being out all night.'

'I'm glad it was edible.' Phylly said, drying up a dish from the drainer. 'Florrie's such a good cook and I didn't want to let her down.'

'You did a fine job.'

Phylly had stepped in to cook breakfast for Jacob and Ned so that Florrie, with her husband's encouragement, could get ready and still go on her long-planned trip to see her sister. Florrie had taken some persuading and had finally agreed to go, but only after she'd satisfied herself that her husband and son were safe and unharmed, and just in need of some food and a nap.

By the time Florrie had left to catch her bus, both men were hungrily tucking into a plateful of fried eggs, bacon and tomatoes, with plenty of bread and butter and a mug of tea.

'What time did the guards come back?' Phylly asked, glad that she could finally start on the many questions that were buzzing around her mind.

Jacob and Ned had explained about the guards

stealing red army petrol and removing the dye so they could sell it on the black market before Florrie left, but they hadn't told them all the details. Phylly didn't want to pester them with questions while they ate, so she'd had to wait patiently until they'd finished before she could satisfy her curiosity.

'It was the early hours of the morning,' Ned said. 'Feels a lot longer when you're waiting, though. The platoon had the whole area staked out, watching the track, in the wood and surrounding the gamekeeper's hut.'

'Were they filtering the petrol?'

'We caught them at it red-handed,' Jacob said. 'They had no idea we were there.'

'Why'd they do it?' Phylly asked.

'They got greedy, I suppose.' Jacob shook his head. 'They should have been happy with the job they had – there's plenty of other soldiers who would happily swap their jobs for looking after POWs.'

'Horrible that they were making money out of the war, when most people are pulling together and working hard to get us through this,' Phylly said. 'I never did like that guard.'

'It's a good job Jimmy spotted they were up to something,' Ned said. 'The police had no idea what was going on.'

'I think Benedict and Roberto might have known something. They hinted at it but were too frightened to say anything,' Phylly said. 'They're safe from the horrible guard now, so they might tell me.'

'They'll be a bit late this morning,' Jacob said. 'Now they're short of a driver and guard!'

'I'd better get back to the orchard,' Phylly said, stacking the last clean bowl onto the pile of others that she'd just dried. 'Or the wasps will get more plums than we will.'

'We'll be out to help later,' Ned said, stifling a yawn. 'The state we're in we're more likely to fall asleep on the ladder, so we'd better have sleep first.'

But before any of them could move, the back door burst open and Bea rushed in, her face milk-white and her eyes brimming with tears.

'Bea, whatever is the matter?' Phylly pulled out a chair from the table and quickly ushered Bea to sit down on it.

'I . . . met the postman . . . in the village.' Bea held out an envelope in her hand. 'He had a letter for me. It's from . . . ' She stopped, her face crumpling up as she started to cry.

Phylly fished her handkerchief out of her dungarees pocket and handed it to Bea, then put her arms around the older woman's shaking shoulders.

Bea took it and dabbed at her eyes, fighting hard to try and calm herself. Biting her bottom lip, she took a deep shuddering breath and spoke in a hoarse voice. 'It's about Aunt Min . . . she's died.'

Chapter Seven

Phylly measured out three teaspoons of sugar into a cup of tea and gave it a thorough stir before putting it down in front of Bea.

'Drink up, it'll help with the shock.'

She watched as Bea took several slow sips, her features gradually softening as the warm, sweet tea took effect. Phylly was desperate to ask Bea the question that was burning on her lips, and from the look on Ned's and Jacob's faces, they were anxious to know what had happened to Aunt Min, too. How had she died?

It was Ned who spoke first. 'Was it one of them doodlebugs?'

Bea put her cup down, shaking her head. 'No, not that, thank goodness. The letter's from her neighbour, she says that Aunt Min died in her sleep, from natural causes according to the doctor. She was well into her seventies.'

Phylly slumped down on to a chair, blinking back tears. 'If only she'd stayed here and not gone back . . . '

'It might not have made any difference,' Bea said.

'The fresh air and better food might have helped—' Phylly began.

Bea touched Phylly's arm. 'I know it's hard to take in that she's gone but . . . ' her voice cracked and she paused to compose herself. 'Aunt Min was where she wanted to be. She loved her life in London and it wasn't right for her to stay here.'

'What about Jimmy?' Ned stood up and started pacing back and forth. 'What will happen to him now?'

'Poor lad's going to be heartbroken,' Jacob said. 'He didn't want her to go back because he was frightened she'd be hurt by a doodlebug.' He shook his head. 'We never imagined this was going to happen.'

'Yes, but what's going to happen to Jimmy now?' Ned stopped pacing and sighed. 'Aunt Min was all the family he had left and now she's gone. Will they come and take him away and put him in an orphanage?'

Bea slammed the palm of her hand down hard on the table, making the tea slosh about in her cup. 'Not while I'm here to stop them!' Two pink spots appeared on her pale cheeks. 'He's under our care here as an evacuee, so by my reckoning that means he should stay here at least for the duration.'

'And afterwards?' Ned asked. 'What then?'

Bea pursed her lips. 'We shall see, but I won't let him go into an orphanage without a fight, not when he could have a family and home here with us for as long as he wants.'

'Should we send word to Florrie?' Jacob asked. 'She was fond of Aunt Min and wanted her to stay here.'

'No,' Bea shook her head. 'Leave her to enjoy herself while she can because she'll find out soon enough, and there's nothing she can do to change it. We shouldn't spoil her time with her sister.'

'When are we going to tell Jimmy?' Phylly asked. 'Should we go and fetch him home from school?'

'Aunt Min wouldn't have wanted him to miss out on any schooling. We'll wait, and I'll tell him when he comes home this afternoon . . . but it's not going to be easy, poor lad's already lost both his parents and now Aunt Min . . .'

Phylly felt emotionally shaken up as she walked down to the orchard, ready to start work. She'd liked Aunt Min very much and been impressed by how close she and Jimmy were; their relationship had been rock-solid with much love and respect on both sides. It had shown her that not all families were like hers, not every aunt was as cold and harsh as hers had been when she'd taken in Phylly and her twin brother, John, after their mother died. At least she and John had had each other but Jimmy had no one, no brother or sister to look out for him – he was quite alone in the world.

Phylly sniffed and brushed away tears with the back of her hand. He might not have any blood relatives alive any more, but Jimmy had her and everyone else at Catchetts Farm to look out for him. They all cared about him and would carry on looking after him together for as long as they could. However long that might prove to be.

The cheerful sound of singing greeted Phylly as she walked into the orchard: wonderful '*O Sole Mio*', the first song that Benedict and Roberto had taught her not long after they'd first arrived at the farm. Since Gracie had become friends with them, she too had learned the words and was joining in now with her clear, strong voice as the three of them picked plums. The music gladdened Phylly's heart and gave her strength for what she now had to do.

'Is very sad,' Benedict said after Phylly had broken the news to her friends. 'She good lady, very kind to Jimmy.'

Phylly nodded and squeezed Benedict's arm. 'She was indeed, and she was so pleased that Jimmy's settled and happy here.'

'He won't be when he finds out about Aunt Min,' Gracie said. 'We must all do our best to help him.'

'We will,' Phylly agreed. 'He didn't want to go to school this morning because Jacob and Ned hadn't come back. Jimmy was desperate to find out what happened last night.'

'Have they told you what happened?' Gracie asked. 'I didn't think Ned looked like he wanted to answer questions when he came down here earlier, so I didn't ask, even though I wanted to.'

Phylly smiled at her friend, who had shown great restraint when Ned had coming rushing into the orchard earlier that morning, asking if one of them would come into the kitchen and take over from Florrie for a while so that she would go on her planned visit to her sisters. 'They did once they'd got a good breakfast inside them.'

'Well . . . ?' Gracie urged. 'Spill the beans, then.'

They all listened avidly as Phylly filled them in on the guards' illegal activities and Ned and Jacob's night-time vigil.

'Jimmy is clever to find out what they do,' Benedict said after he'd translated everything Phylly had told them into Italian for Roberto. 'Is good they catched now.'

'Did you know what the guards were doing?' Gracie asked.

Benedict shrugged his shoulders. 'Some. We see them take petrol and creep out in dark. We no say about it because we scared.'

'They'd probably have hurt you if you'd spoken out,' Phylly said. 'It was best someone else found out about it.' She smiled. 'So how were the new driver and guard this morning?'

'Good,' Benedict said. 'We all happy.'

'After what happened to the other two I should imagine all the camp guards will be on their best behaviour now and grateful that they've got a cushy war job compared with many men.' Gracie sighed. 'Come on, we'd better get back to work – those plums won't pick themselves, but the wasps will *help* themselves.'

Back at work, with Phylly now joining in with the picking, Benedict began to sing a gentle-sounding Italian song, one which she hadn't heard before. She had no idea what the words meant, but the song was soothing and just what they probably all needed as they worked, their minds absorbed with all that had recently happened, both the good and the bad.

'Phylly, is there anything you'd especially like me to pack for your picnic tonight?' Bea asked when she brought the snack and drink for them later that morning.

'Picnic?' Phylly asked.

'For you and Edwin,' Bea reminded her. 'I thought you were going to show him Yaxley castle?'

'Yes, of course . . . I'd forgotten about it with everything that's been going on.' Phylly bit her bottom lip. 'Perhaps we should call it off, it wouldn't be right to go out enjoying ourselves with Aunt Min dying.'

Bea touched Phylly's arm. 'You should go. Aunt Min

wouldn't have wanted you to cancel it, and I'm sure Edwin's really looking forward to it. He needs to do fun things when he can – you know how it is with the airmen when they're not on missions, they all live life to the full and enjoy themselves because . . . they don't know what tomorrow will bring. Don't disappoint him by calling it off tonight, Phylly.' She blinked back tears. 'Go and remember Aunt Min with happiness. So, what would you like in the picnic?'

'As long as you're sure it wouldn't be disrespectful, then can we please take some of your scones? Edwin loves them.'

'Of course, I'll put some butter and jam in as well.' Bea smiled at her then turned to speak to Gracie. 'You wanted to ask me something about Richard's socks?'

Leaving them to talk about knitting the heels of socks, Phylly wandered over to sit in the shade with Benedict and Roberto.

'You and Edwin . . . together?' Benedict asked Phylly quietly. 'You love him?'

Phylly nearly choked on her mouthful of cold tea.

'No, we're *not* together, we just like each other's company and are good friends. Nothing more.'

Benedict looked her straight in the eyes, his blue eyes twinkling. 'You make lovely couple. I think he like you.'

Phylly smiled. 'Honestly, Benedict, we are *just friends*.'

'I think you like him here,' Benedict laid a hand over his heart and beamed at her. 'He same for you. I see it. Is good.'

'You Italians are so romantic.' Phylly laughed. 'But I can assure you there isn't any romance between myself and Edwin.'

Benedict shrugged. 'Could be if you let it . . . '

But I'm *not* going to let it, Phylly thought. It was far too risky to let herself fall in love again, even with Edwin.

Jimmy looked at the clock on the classroom wall. It had barely moved since he last checked. He sighed. Today felt like the longest day he'd ever spent at school: every minute, every second seemed to take ten times as long to pass. The more he looked at the clock, the slower it seemed to go.

Keep busy, that's what Aunt Min always said if you wanted to forget about something, occupy yourself to take your mind off it. With a final glance at the clock, which was hardly any further on, Jimmy applied himself to his work and carefully marked the countries which the teacher had listed on the blackboard onto his map. He concentrated hard, focusing on getting it right because he liked learning about different places. His dad used to tell him stories about the countries he'd been to, and one day Jimmy hoped he'd get to see some of those places for himself. For now, he had to get the map right, putting Australia and New Zealand in the correct place to start with.

Following Aunt Min's advice worked because the rest of the afternoon passed quickly and he was relieved when the teacher told the class to put away their maps because it was time to go home. Jimmy was ready and waiting quicker than he'd ever been before, sitting up straight, eager for them to be dismissed. Even when they were free to go he still had to hold on and walk out of the door and across the playground, but the moment he was through the gate he ran – going as fast as his legs would carry him, he raced through the village and took the road back to Catchetts Farm.

His mind was racing too, feeling like it was ready to burst as it seethed with all the questions he had for Jacob and Ned. Which should he ask first? Did they camouflage themselves? Was the whole Home Guard platoon there?

Sprinting into the farmyard, he caught sight of Ned working in one of the barns so instead of going straight to the house as he normally would after school, he rushed over to him.

'Ned!' he panted, putting his hands on his knees and bending over for a few moments to catch his breath.

'Hello, Jimmy, are you all right?'

Jimmy nodded as he stood up straight and then started firing off his questions. 'What time did the guards come back? Did they put up a fight?'

'I'll tell you about it another time. You need to come

indoors for a bit first.' Ned put a hand on Jimmy's shoulder and steered him out of the barn and across the yard towards the house.

'Why?' Jimmy looked up at Ned's face – it looked odd, as if he was very uncomfortable. 'What's the matter? What's going on?' He couldn't understand why Ned was being like this. He should be glad about what happened last night, shouldn't he?

The kitchen was full of the warmth and mouth-watering smell of baking. Piles of scones were cooling on racks on the wooden table and Bea was busy rolling out pastry, but she stopped at the sight of Jimmy and Ned.

'Jimmy!' Bea smiled at him, but her voice sounded odd. 'Come and sit down.' She pulled out a chair for him and beckoned him to sit, then went over to the sink to wash her hands.

An uneasy feeling crept through Jimmy; something peculiar was going on. What was the matter with everyone this afternoon? Why were they acting strange and looking so ill at ease?

'You go back to work, Ned, while I talk to Jimmy.' Bea pulled out a chair and sat down beside him.

Ned patted Jimmy's shoulder then went back outside without saying a word. Jimmy watched him go and started to stand up to follow him out in a bid to get answers to his questions.

'Wait!' Bea grabbed both his hands in hers and gently settled him back down on the chair.

'What's going . . . ' Jimmy began and stopped when he noticed how pale and strained Bea's face looked – it was as if she wanted to cry.

'What's the matter?' he asked.

Bea held his hands tighter. 'We've had some bad news today.' She paused and swallowed hard, her blue eyes meeting his. 'I'm sorry to tell you that Aunt Min has died.'

Jimmy stared at her. He must have misheard her. He saw her lips move and the words come out, but they didn't make sense.

'Do you understand what I'm telling you? Aunt Min's neighbour wrote to me to say that she'd died in her sleep from natural causes.'

'No!' Jimmy shook his head, trying to get those awful words out of his mind. 'It can't be true.'

'I'm sorry, but it is.'

The world felt as if it had suddenly tipped on its side and everything had altered. His lips felt numb and his stomach had plummeted to the floor. How could this be true? Just minutes ago, he'd been running home from school, bursting to talk to Ned and Jacob about last night . . . and now *this* . . . Bea was saying that Aunt Min was dead, but she couldn't be, she said she'd come back to see him soon – she'd promised.

Jimmy stood up, pushing his chair back so hard it made a harsh scraping noise against the tiled floor.

'It's not true!' he shouted, running out of the kitchen at full pelt.

'Jimmy!' Bea called after him, but he didn't look back.

The sharp tang of tomato plants met Jimmy as he opened the large greenhouse door and slipped inside where it was quiet and he could be alone. He turned a wooden crate upside down and sat down on it, slumping forward with his elbows on his knees and his chin cupped in his hand, and started to try and work out what was going on.

Aunt Min couldn't be dead, he reasoned, so why would Bea tell him she was? It wasn't the sort of thing you would lie about. He scuffed at the earth floor with his boot, twisting his foot from side to side, making a pattern in the soil. Slowly, so slowly, the meaning of Bea's words were gradually sinking in. Jimmy shook his head as a monstrous surge of sadness swept through him, making him shake and gulp as sobs erupted out of him.

'Jimmy?'

He looked up and saw Jacob standing beside him, twine and his pocket knife in his hand. 'I was tying up some stray tomato vines down the other end.' He nodded towards the far end of the long greenhouse. He crouched down so that his face was level with Jimmy's. 'They've told you about Aunt Min, then?'

'It can't be true . . .' Jimmy's voice came out

strangely squeaky because of the huge lump that had wedged itself in his throat.

'I'm afraid it is.'

More hot tears slid down Jimmy's face. 'She shouldn't have gone back . . . Florrie said she could stay here . . . ' He gulped, his chest heaving as more sobs forced their way out. 'I wanted her to stay.'

Jacob patted Jimmy's shoulder. 'I don't think it would have mattered where she was if it was her time to go. At least it was peaceful for her.'

They sat quietly for a few minutes as Jimmy cried his tears out. He'd heard all that Bea and now Jacob had said – they wouldn't lie to him, so it must be true. Aunt Min had died. It didn't seem real that she was gone, and he wouldn't see her any more, that he wouldn't go home to her after the war as they'd planned.

Jimmy's stomach lurched as he thought about this. Where would he go then – to an orphanage?

'What will happen to me, Jacob?'

'You'll stay here with us, of course.'

'But what about after the war when all the other

children go back home to their families? I haven't got one to go back to any more.'

The sound of joyful singing could still be heard after the truck had left the farmyard and was bumping its way down the lane to the road. Phylly smiled – she loved the way the Italian POWs sang together, their voices harmonising over the beautiful sounding words. Benedict and Roberto were always the last to be picked up, and the almost-full truck of POWs had been in a jubilant mood tonight and were singing loudly when they'd arrived at Catchetts Farm; they'd probably carry on all the way back to their camp in relief and celebration that their lives would no longer be tormented by the two guards.

Phylly checked the time on her watch. She'd better get a move on if she was going to be ready for when Edwin arrived. He'd been promised the loan of a jeep so they'd planned to visit the ruins of Yaxley castle to indulge his love of old British buildings.

Up in the bedroom which she shared with Gracie, Phylly washed off the dirt, dust and stickiness from a day's plum-picking and it felt good to be clean again.

She changed into her one and only dress, the same one she'd worn for the Hundredth Mission dance, then brushed her wavy blonde hair and secured it at the sides with clips. She was applying a final touch of the precious red lipstick which Edwin's mother, Annie, had sent over from America, when Gracie walked in holding her knitting.

'Oh, you look lovely,' Gracie said. 'You should wear that dress more often – the colour really suits you.'

'Thank you.' Phylly bobbed a curtsey. 'There's not much call for wearing your best dress when you're a Land Girl picking plums or hoeing weeds.' She checked her reflection in the mirror standing on top of the chest of drawers and, satisfied that her lips were red enough, put the tube of lipstick away in her drawer.

'You know, from the amount of care you're taking getting ready anyone might think you're sweet on Edwin and that you like him as much as he likes you.'

Phylly turned around to look at Gracie who had sat down on her bed and was knitting the foot part of a sock for which Bea had done the heel that afternoon.

'We're. Just. Friends. How many times do I have to tell you that before you believe me, Gracie? I'm looking nice for me and no one else and it feels good to be wearing something other than Land Army uniform.'

Gracie shrugged. 'If you say so, Phylly.' She grinned. 'But you would make a lovely couple given the chance.'

'Very funny. Concentrate on your knitting instead of trying to match me up with Edwin.' Phylly grabbed her cardigan and made for the door. 'I'll see you later.'

Downstairs in the kitchen, Bea had a packed basket ready for her.

'There are some freshly baked scones, butter and jam in there. I know how much Edwin likes them,' Bea said.

'Thank you, you do spoil him,' Phylly said, lifting the cloth covering the basket and peeping inside.

'He deserves it. I'm doing it for my friend Annie, too – she'd be baking scones for him if she was here,' Bea sighed. 'But she's not, so I'm doing it for her.'

Phylly picked up the basket. 'I'm sure she appreciates what you're doing for her son and perhaps one day you'll get to see each other again.'

Bea smiled. 'I hope so. Now we know what happened to her maybe she'll swallow her stubborn pride and come home to see us when this crazy war is over.'

She glanced at her watch. 'Edwin should be here soon. I'll walk down and meet him on the road. Thanks for the picnic.'

'Just make sure Edwin eats plenty.'

'There'll be no doubt about that when he sees those scones,' Phylly said. 'I'll see you later.'

Outside it was a beautiful September evening, still warm enough but with a softer, gentle heat as swallows darted across the sky, their chattering calls filling the air. Phylly swung the basket as she walked down the lane, glad to stretch out her legs after a day of mostly standing on ladders. The thought of the evening ahead exploring the old castle ruins and sharing a picnic with Edwin made her smile – he was always such good company, so courteous and interesting to talk to.

Reaching the end of the lane, she left the basket on the ground and climbed up to sit on top of the five-bar wooden gate, from where she had a good view over the hedgetops and would be able to see Edwin coming. Closing her eyes for a moment she breathed in deeply, inhaling the rich, sweet scent of the honeysuckle growing in the hedge, and listened to the sounds of the countryside all around her, the birds twittering and the drone of insects. In moments like this it was hard to believe that there was a war going on. Phylly sighed and opened her eyes. She wished it was true, that it was over and everyone could be at peace again. No more fighting – no more killing.

Although she didn't like the war, it had changed her life for good in many ways. She was doing work she'd never have been able to do before, living in a place she loved, had made friends with Gracie and all those living at the farm and met people from foreign places: Benedict, Roberto and of course Edwin. It hadn't been all bad, and it had taught them all to make the most of every day, because you never knew what was around the corner. You snatched what enjoyment you could, times like tonight when her tired body would rather have just laid on her bed and read a book all evening, but that would be wasting an opportunity to go out and have fun while she could.

Edwin was late. He should have been there half an hour ago. Phylly jumped down from her perch on top of the gate and rubbed the back of her legs which had become numb from sitting up there for so long. Had he forgotten? Or perhaps he'd had to go on an unexpected mission and couldn't get word to her as there wasn't a telephone at the farm. She decided not to wait there any longer as she was hungry after a hard day's work. If Edwin was just late, then she'd meet him back at the farmhouse.

Phylly was sitting at the table having something to eat with everyone else when she heard the sound of a jeep pulling into the yard. It sent her heart leaping with relief that Edwin was finally here and they would be going to the castle after all.

'Better late than never,' she said, getting up from the

table, grabbing her cardigan and the picnic basket and making for the door. 'I'll see you later.'

Walking outside into the bright evening sunshine of the yard, Phylly's eyes were dazzled for a moment after the dimmer light of the kitchen.

'Did you forget the time or—' she stopped when she saw who it was getting out of the jeep. It wasn't Edwin, but Charlie, one of his friends who she'd met at the Hundredth Mission dance. Phylly's stomach clenched as an ice-cold feeling shivered through her.

Charlie took off his cap as he came towards her. 'Hello, Phylly.'

'Where's Edwin? Is he all right?'

Charlie cleared his throat. 'I'm sorry to tell you that Edwin didn't come back from his last mission yesterday.'

Phylly stared at him for a few moments and then somehow found her voice. 'What happened?'

'I can't tell you much yet, only that his plane was hit and losing height. We don't know for sure what did happen.' He paused, twisting his cap in his hands.

'Edwin asked me to come and tell you if anything happened to him.'

Phylly nodded. 'What about Edwin's mother?'

'She'll have been informed by telegram.' Charlie reached out and touched her arm. 'I know this is a shock. Is there anything I can do for you, Phylly?'

'No. Thank you.' Phylly swallowed hard. 'I appreciate you coming to tell me, I wouldn't have known otherwise.'

'I promise I'll come back and see you as soon as I know any more.' He put on his cap and climbed back in the jeep. 'Goodbye – take care.' With a final wave he drove off.

Phylly stared after him, standing motionless as she listened to the jeep's engine going down the lane to the road and eventually fading away into the distance, leaving just the familiar sounds of the farmyard – the house martins swooping overhead and the buzz of bees around Florrie's flowers.

'Phylly! You're still here!' Gracie's voice made her jump. 'Why didn't you go with Edwin?'

'It wasn't him.' Phylly's voice sounded odd. 'It was his friend, Charlie . . . he came to tell me . . . ' Her voice cracked. 'Edwin's . . . plane was hit – it went down.'

Phylly couldn't sleep. She'd lain wide awake since she and Gracie had come to bed at ten o'clock. Gracie had soon fallen asleep, but there'd been no relief or escape for Phylly – her mind was too full of questions with no answers, only her imagination racing ahead painting numerous scenarios of what might have happened to Edwin.

She threw back her covers, padded over to the window and parted the blackout curtains to look down into Florrie's walled garden which was bathed in moonlight, painting everything in shades of grey. The memory of the day when Edwin had told them he was the son of Bea's best friend down there in the garden came back to Phylly. It had been a big surprise but since then he'd slipped effortlessly into all their lives, becoming a good friend and frequent and most welcome visitor to the farm. The thought that he might never come back again was too much, she couldn't stop a loud sob bursting out of her.

'Phylly?' Gracie's muffled voice startled her.

'It's all right, go back to sleep,' Phylly managed, biting down the rising tide of emotion that threatened to spill out.

Gracie ignored her and got out of bed. 'I remember how hard it is to sleep after getting news like that.' She took hold of both of Phylly's hands in hers. 'Edwin's plane might have landed, or he bailed out. Hold on to that. That's what you told me to do, and you were right.'

'But . . . '

'Come on, let's go and make some cocoa, it'll help you sleep.'

They discovered that they weren't the only ones who couldn't sleep – Bea was sitting at the kitchen table nursing a cup of tea. She'd drawn back the curtains and the room was bathed in eerie moonlight, which drained all the colour from everything and made the world look as sad as Phylly felt.

'Phylly! Gracie! What's the matter?' Bea asked.

'We need some cocoa,' Gracie said.

'I'll make some for you.' Bea went to stand up.

'No, no, I'll do it.' Gracie pulled out a chair and steered Phylly to sit down.

'Couldn't you sleep either?' Phylly asked.

Bea shook her head. 'I keep thinking about Annie. She'll have heard Edwin didn't come back from his mission – what must she be feeling so far away and not a thing she can do but wait?'

'And hope,' Gracie said spooning cocoa powder into two cups. 'There's always hope.'

Bea nodded. 'Of course there is. We mustn't give up hope that Edwin's alive, like your Richard and . . . ' Bea's voice cracked. She sighed deeply shaking her head. 'What a day we've had – first the news about Aunt Min, having to tell Jimmy the last member of his family has gone, and then Edwin being missing. What's going to happen next? What will become of us all in this horrible, awful, stupid war?' Fat tears trickled down Bea's face.

Phylly grabbed hold of Bea's hand. 'It'll be all right in the end, Bea, you'll see. We'll get through it.'

But would they, Phylly thought? Would they really?

Chapter Eight

The steady clip-clop of the horse's hooves made Phylly sleepy and she was having trouble keeping her eyes open. She'd gone with Ned to take boxes of fruit and vegetables to the nearest railway station and now they were on their way back to the farm.

'You nodding off?' Ned's voice jolted her awake.

'Sorry, didn't get much sleep last night.' She'd finally managed a few hours after her and Gracie's late-night chat in the kitchen with Bea, but it hadn't been enough and she felt very tired and out of sorts today, her thoughts constantly returning to Edwin and worrying over his fate. Was he alive, or not?

'Bea told me you were up in the night. I thought bringing you out for a change of scene might help.' He smiled at her. 'Gracie and the POWs can manage on their own for a while, how about taking the rest of the day off?'

Phylly shook her head. 'It's kind of you to offer, but there's work to do. People still need feeding whether someone's gone missing or not, and me moping around won't help Edwin. It's best to keep busy.'

They fell into silence for a while, looking out across the hedgetops from their high seat in the trap – while above them, hidden by the overcast cloud, they could hear the drone as American planes flew off on yet another bombing raid.

'There they go again,' Ned said. 'The sky always full of aeroplanes, day or night.'

'But not Edwin's plane any more,' Phylly sighed. 'You know, he wanted me to be his girl,' she blurted out, 'but I turned him down.'

She looked down at her hands clasped tightly in her lap, her knuckles standing out white against her skin. She'd needed to tell someone about what had happened as it had been eating away at her since the news had come about Edwin's plane going down. Now she couldn't shake off the awful feeling that she'd been wrong to wait. She should've grabbed the chance to be together and the happiness it would have brought them while they could.

'Why'd you do that?' Ned asked, gently. 'You liked the fellow, didn't you?'

'Yes, very much. But I was wary of loving anyone again after losing my fiancé at Dunkirk . . . knowing that they could be snatched away at any moment . . . especially with Edwin flying missions over enemy territory. I couldn't face going through that again.' She sighed. 'Edwin couldn't persuade me to change my mind, so we agreed to wait until he'd finished his missions and then he was going to volunteer to do a ground-based job instead of going back to America with the rest of his crew. It would have been safer to be together then.'

Ned nodded. 'They're all fair reasons.'

'But maybe we were wrong! I can't help thinking we should've snatched what happiness we could while we had the chance . . . ' Phylly's voice cracked and she stopped to compose herself. 'Now we might never get the chance if . . . if Edwin doesn't come back.'

'It's hard to choose when your head tells you to do one thing, but your heart wants you to do the opposite. Which of them is right?' Ned paused. 'Remember I did a similar thing by not telling Edwin's mother, Annie, how I felt? It was only me holding back because she never knew that I loved her, and I didn't say anything for what I thought was a good reason . . . then it was too late. I missed my chance.'

Phylly patted his arm. 'We're a right cautious pair, aren't we?'

'It comes out of caring for other people. War heightens emotions and speeds everything up, makes every moment precious. It's no wonder many people grab at any chance of joy they get because you just don't know—'

'I wish I could go back. I'd listen to my heart for

once and grab my chance with Edwin just like he wanted.' Phylly shook her head sadly. 'But nothing can turn back time.'

'You might still get your chance to do what your heart tells you. It could happen.'

'I hope so.' Phylly smiled. 'I'm hoping and hoping – it's all I can do.'

'What did you do today?' Bea tipped a pile of chopped onions into the pan, where they started to gently sizzle in the heat.

Jimmy shrugged. 'Just more sums.'

He stood beside Bea watching her stir the glistening onions, glad to be back home with her. He hadn't wanted to go to school today but Bea had insisted that he did, saying that Aunt Min wouldn't have wanted him to miss his education. He'd gone for Aunt Min, because he knew how important it was to her, but it had been a long, hard day and he'd found it impossible to concentrate on what he was supposed to be doing. Practising long multiplication sums had no appeal when all he'd been able to think about was that Aunt Min was gone and that he'd never see her again.

When the school day had finally ended he'd come straight home, back to the farmhouse, back to Bea and he'd stayed close by her side since then. Usually when he got home he'd come in for a drink and something to eat, then go out and to find Ned or Jacob, or the Land Girls and POWs, and join in with whatever they were doing, but not today. Jimmy needed to stay close to Bea.

'Here,' Bea handed him the spoon she'd been using to stir the onions. 'You take over for me while I cut up the meat. All right?'

Jimmy nodded and started to stir the onions around.

'That's it, keep them moving so they don't burn, we just need to soften them up.' Bea squeezed his shoulder and went over to chop up more ingredients at the table.

Jimmy concentrated on what he was doing, making patterns in the glistening onions as he moved the spoon in different directions.

'Hello, I'm home!'

The voice made Jimmy jump. He turned around to see Florrie standing in the kitchen door, a wide smile lighting up her face. She put down her bag and came over to see what he was doing.

'You're doing a good job there,' Florrie said looking over his shoulder. 'I've been telling my sister all about you and how well you've settled in here. She's going to come and see us one of these days because her evacuees have gone home again, couldn't stand the quiet of the countryside. She said—'

'Mum.' Bea touched Florrie's arm. 'I need to talk to you.'

'What's the matter?' Florrie asked, her face full of concern. 'What's going on?'

'Sit down and I'll be there in a moment.' Bea added pieces of rabbit meat into the pan with the onions. 'You need to brown the meat now, Jimmy, turn each bit over so every side gets cooked, can you do that?'

Jimmy nodded. He knew what was coming and turned his back on Bea and Florrie, focusing his attention on browning the rabbit meat just as Bea had instructed.

'Oh no!' Florrie gasped when Bea had told her the news. 'Poor Min.'

Jimmy heard a chair being pushed backwards fast and felt Florrie's warm arms wrap around him, hugging him tightly against her lavender-scented shoulder.

'Oh, Jimmy. I'm so, so sorry.' Florrie's voice was thick with tears.

'That's not all,' Bea said. 'I'm afraid there's more bad news.' She told Florrie about Edwin being missing.

Jimmy felt Florrie's body stiffen as the second lot of bad news hit her. She hugged him tighter for a few moments, then loosened her arms and put her hands on his shoulders, turning him to face her.

'There's nothing I can do to help Edwin, he's in God's hands now, and I hope He sends him back to us – but as for you, Jimmy,' she smiled at him, her kind blue eyes, bright with tears, 'there's something I can give you that will help.'

'What do you mean?' Bea asked.

'You'll see.' Florrie hurried out of door and they could hear her footsteps tip-tapping up the stairs.

Bea looked at Jimmy and shrugged. 'Let's have a look at how that meat's doing.'

Florrie returned a few minutes later carrying an envelope. 'It's for you.' She handed it to Bea.

'What is it?' Bea stared at her name written on the front.

'It's from Aunt Min. She gave it to me when she came here . . . go on, open it.'

Jimmy watched as Bea opened the envelope, took out a single sheet of paper and read the words, which he could see were written in Aunt Min's distinctive handwriting.

'Oh my!' Bea gasped, her eyes bright with tears. 'Look, Jimmy, Mum.' She held out the letter for them both to read.

'"Dear Bea,"' Jimmy read.

I've given this letter to Florrie, just in case, because none of us knows what's in store for us. Should anything happen to me, I want Jimmy to be well looked after, safe and most importantly happy. I hope, if the need arises that he can stay with you. I've been so impressed with the way you've taken him into your home and your heart. If I'm no longer here to look after Jimmy, then I can think of no finer person than you to do it. Perhaps, if you are willing you could adopt him, become his mother for real?

With my grateful thanks,

Min Pritchard.

'She was a wise woman, your Aunt Min.' Florrie put her arm around Jimmy's shoulders. 'What do you think about Bea becoming your mother for real?'

Jimmy looked at Bea who stood quietly looking at him, her eyes shining brightly. Would he like her to be his mother? He didn't need to think about the answer – he knew it without question – but was it what Bea wanted? She hadn't said a word about what she thought of Aunt Min's suggestion. It was a big thing to take on someone else's child for ever. Looking after an evacuee for the war was one thing, but for ever was a lot to ask of someone.

'What do you think, Bea?' Jimmy asked.

'I think it's a good idea,' she said quietly, 'but only if you agree that it's what *you* want.' She paused and smiled. '*If* it is what you want, then I'd be delighted to become your mother.'

Jimmy nodded and grinned. 'Yes, please!' He flung himself into Bea's arms and hugged her tightly.

Aunt Min was gone but she'd made sure that he was safe, cared-for and loved.

November 1944

Chapter Nine

Jimmy didn't want to go. Not any more. When Edwin had first told him about Thanksgiving, way back in the summer, he'd promised Jimmy that he'd take him to celebrate it with the other Americans at his airbase. It sounded wonderful and he'd been delighted at the thought of going, but now the day was here, and his school had been invited to the nearby American airbase to celebrate, he didn't want to go. Not without Edwin.

'Come on, Jimmy, hurry up or you'll be late for school,' Phylly's voice called.

'Good.' Jimmy sat on his bed, his arms folded firmly

across the front of his new blue pullover, which Bea had knitted him.

The door opened and Phylly peered inside. 'You look nice in that jumper . . . what's the matter, Jimmy?'

'I'm not going.'

'You're not going? 'Phylly came in and knelt down beside him.

Jimmy shook his head.

'Don't you like roast turkey and ice cream then?'

'I do . . . '

Phylly shrugged. 'It'll be a pity to miss out on them, won't it? All the other children are going – do you want to be the only one that isn't there and misses all the fun and delicious food?'

Jimmy's throat tightened. 'I can't go.'

Phylly took hold of his hands in hers. 'Why not?'

'Because . . . Edwin's not going to be there.' A sob spilled out of him and somehow he found himself crying in Phylly's arms.

'Hush,' she said softly, holding him tight. 'It's all right.'

'He . . . said . . . he'd . . . take . . . us . . . to . . . Thanksgiving.' Jimmy managed through his sobs.

'I remember.'

Phylly's voice sounded strange and Jimmy pulled out of his arms and looked at her – she had tears in her eyes.

'Don't cry, Phylly.' He did his best to smile at her.

'I'm all right.' Phylly sniffed. 'We all miss him, don't we?'

Jimmy nodded. 'Do you think he'll come back?'

Phylly shrugged. 'I don't know. It's been weeks since his plane went down but I hope he's out there somewhere and we'll see him again one day.' She stood up and smoothed a hand over Jimmy's neatly combed hair. 'Come on, let's go.'

Should he go, or not? Jimmy wondered. He hesitated, torn between wanting to go and yet feeling that he'd be betraying Edwin by going without him.

Phylly held out her hand to him. 'Edwin would want you to go and enjoy yourself.'

'Do you think so?'

'I *know* so. He'd be sorry if you missed out on today.'

Jimmy stood up and took her hand. He'd go for Edwin.

'He loves his socks!' Gracie shrieked as she read her husband's latest letter, which the postman had delivered that morning. 'He's amazed that I've learned to knit and has put in an order for a balaclava next. Do you think I could manage that, Bea?'

'Of course you can.' Bea smiled as she poured tea into the cups lined up on the table.

Now the weather had turned colder, the Land Girls and POWs usually came into the farmhouse for their morning break as it gave them a chance to warm up again.

'Socks special because you make them with love.' Benedict sat down at the kitchen table and warmed his hands around his cup of tea. 'He knows this.'

Gracie beamed at him. 'Lots of love and a great deal of patience. I'm so happy that he likes them.'

'I make this for you.' Benedict took a small wooden heart out of his pocket and handed it to Gracie. 'For you send him your heart.'

Gracie stroked the small, perfectly shaped heart, which had been polished to a silky smoothness, emphasising the wood's beautiful grain pattern. 'Oh, thank you, Benedict, this is . . . ' She blinked back tears. 'This is beautiful.'

'Is like mine.' He took a half of a similar wooden heart out of his pocket and showed her. 'Maddalena, my wife, she have other half. I make heart for you in two bits.'

Gracie saw that her own wooden heart had a fine line running around it and she gently pulled the two pieces apart, one for her to keep and one to send to Richard. 'Benedict . . . for once I don't know what to say. Thank you very much.'

Benedict bowed his head and placed his hand on his heart.

'You welcome, Gracie. This war, can no stop love.'

Gracie's eyes blurred with tears. 'You're right. Even if we're miles apart the love doesn't stop. One day we'll all be together again, you and Maddalena, and Richard and me.'

*

Jimmy had never seen so much food in one place before. The long tables were groaning with platters of different foods, many of which he'd never seen before, and had no idea what they were.

'Help yourself,' said the serviceman who was standing in the queue behind Jimmy. 'There's plenty to go around.'

Holding his plate in front of him, Jimmy didn't know where to start. Most of his classmates didn't have the same problem and were already helping themselves, piling food onto their plates. 'I'm not sure . . . '

'What's your name?' the American asked. 'I'm Buddy.'

'It's Jimmy.'

'OK then, Jimmy, let me help you. First off, you can't have a Thanksgiving dinner without turkey, then you should have some creamed potato, cornbread . . . '

Buddy guided him along the serving table, explaining what each food was and recommending what to try. Jimmy remembered his good manners, saying please and thank you when he was offered something, and Buddy added it to their plates.

Jimmy's plate quickly filled up with food, some of which he had no idea what it would taste like, but he was willing to try it because the Americans had gone to a great deal of trouble to make the magnificent dinner for them.

Buddy led him over to sit at one of the long tables where children and serviceman were sitting side by side tucking into their food.

'So, did you enjoy your ride here in the truck?' Buddy asked.

'Yes, thank you,' Jimmy said as they sat down next to each other. 'But they had to lift us in because it was so high up, even the teachers needed help.' The Americans had collected them from school in two large, canvas-covered trucks where the children and teachers had sat in back on long benches along each side. 'It was fun riding in one.'

'Good. OK, time to try your first Thanksgiving dinner,' Buddy said. 'Try putting a bit of cranberry sauce on your turkey, it makes it taste real good.'

Jimmy watched as Buddy dipped a piece of turkey

into the red, jam-like sauce before popping it into his mouth, and as he chewed a look of joy spread across his face. Would he like it, too? Jimmy wondered. Turkey with jam wasn't how they ate it in Britain but then they didn't normally celebrate Thanksgiving either. Today was a day to try new things, Jimmy reminded himself. He'd never know what it was like unless he tried it and Edwin had said he liked it, so it must be all right.

'Do you remember what happened the first time I took you home?' Phylly asked as she walked Jimmy back to the farm under an inky-black, starlit sky. She'd met him from school, where the American trucks had returned the children and teachers long past their usual home-time, but it was worth it for the special occasion.

'Of course.' Jimmy's breath came out in a misty plume in the cold night air. 'We had to jump in a ditch after you waved at that German plane.'

'Don't remind me.' Phylly shivered at the thought of what could have happened that day and how stupid she'd been waving at an enemy plane. Luckily for them he'd been friendly and hadn't tried to shoot them, as some planes did.

'That's when we first met Edwin. He nearly ran me over and you were really angry with him.'

Tears stung Phylly's eyes as she remembered how kind and polite Edwin had been, even after she'd shouted at him. He was always so generous-hearted and lovely, so easy to be around and to . . . love. The word slipped so easily into her mind. Just four little letters, but which meant so much. If only he were still here . . . if only he'd come back . . . but there was no news and although the old saying 'no news is good news' was supposed to be cheering, the longer it had been since Edwin went missing, the less likely it seemed that he'd ever come back. Phylly still hoped she'd see him again but her mind had begun to betray her with thoughts that he may be gone for ever. She tried hard to stay positive and hopeful, but sometimes it was so hard.

'I was really scared of going to live at Catchetts Farm,' Jimmy said. 'I thought it would be like the first time I was evacuated and Bea would beat me for being late.'

'She'd never do that.'

'I know that now, but I didn't then.'

'A lot's changed since you arrived. It's only been a few months, but it feels a lot longer in some ways. Things have happened in our lives that we never expected.'

'You mean like Aunt Min dying?'

Phylly put her arm around Jimmy's shoulders and hugged him to her. 'Yes, like Aunt Min dying. She was very proud of you, you know that, don't you? And so glad that you're safe and happy here.'

'I know.' Jimmy's voice wobbled. 'I still miss her.'

'Of course you do, and so you should. She was a big part of your life and you don't get over missing someone who's important to you that quickly.'

'Do you miss Edwin?'

Phylly swallowed hard. 'Yes, I do.'

'The Americans at the Thanksgiving reminded me of him,' Jimmy said. 'They were all kind and polite and called our teachers ma'am, just like Edwin used to call Florrie and Bea.'

'And they put a sort of jam on their turkey,' Jimmy said. 'I wasn't sure about having any, but Buddy said I should try it and I liked it. The Americans call it cranberry sauce.'

Phylly looked around at everyone listening to Jimmy describing the things he'd seen and done at the Thanksgiving celebration. Bea, Florrie, Ned, Jacob and Gracie were all gathered around the table, cosy in the farmhouse kitchen, where the range was filling the room with warmth. These were people whom Phylly hadn't known a few years or even months ago, but now were like family to her. The war was a terrible thing, but it had brought them together – people who otherwise would never have come to know each other and they had shared both difficult and good times. She was glad she was part of it. She treasured times like this, as they helped to ease the terrible ache of missing Edwin for a short while.

'The ice cream we had for afters was made in a B-24 Liberator – they flew it up high enough to make it freeze solid into ice cream,' Jimmy said, 'and it was still frozen when the plane landed.'

'The Americans certainly know how to entertain people,' Florrie said. 'We should invite Buddy and some others over for tea as a thank you.'

'You could make them some scones,' Jimmy said. 'Edwin likes them.'

'Yes, he certainly does,' Florrie said, smiling at Phylly.

'Come on, Jimmy.' Bea stood up. 'If you want me to read the next chapter of *Wind in the Willows* you need to go to bed now, otherwise we'll have to wait until tomorrow night to find out what happens to Mr Toad.'

'I'm coming now. Night, night, everyone.' Jimmy followed Bea out of the door to a chorus of good-night wishes.

Gracie started collecting the last of the plates from the table. 'Let's get the washing up done now, Phylly, I want to be ready when Bea comes down so she can get me started on knitting a balaclava. You wash, and I'll wipe.'

While Phylly washed up she thought about what

Jimmy had told them. It gave her a better understanding of what Edwin's life was like on his airbase. She was finishing the last plate when she heard the sound of a vehicle driving into the farmyard. Pulling back the blackout curtain she peered out but couldn't see much except the weak beams of light coming through the thin gaps in the headlight covers. She couldn't see who it was.

'We're not expecting anyone, are we?' Ned stood up from the table where was working his way through some of the latest government forms that had been sent to the farm and looked out of the window.

'Not that I know of,' Jacob said. 'Could be someone on Home Guard business.' He got up from his chair by the range where he'd been sitting opposite Florrie, who was darning some socks. 'I'll go and see.'

'Go with him, Ned,' Florrie said.

Phylly watched as the two men went outside, taking care to close the door behind them. She could hear raised voices outside and moments later, Ned burst back into the kitchen. 'We've got an American visitor.'

A heavy, sickening feeling flooded through Phylly. Had there been news about Edwin? Had they found out what had happened to him? Had his friend come back to tell them that he was no longer just missing, but confirmed as killed in action?

Phylly closed her eyes and held on to the side of the sink. She heard the door open and the sound of people coming in but didn't dare look. Not yet. These could be the last few precious moments when she could go on hoping that there'd be good news, before it was shattered for ever.

'Edwin!' Florrie's shrieked.

Phylly snapped her eyes open as the small figure of Florrie flew across the kitchen and flung her arms around him. He squeezed her back and then looked up, directly at Phylly, their eyes meeting and holding for what seemed like an age. He smiled at her, his beautiful blue eyes crinkling up at the corners.

'You've lost weight,' Florrie said, loosening her hold on him and stepping back to give him a good look up and down.

Edwin laughed. 'I couldn't get any scones where I've been.'

'We'll soon remedy that.' Florrie took hold of his arm and marched him over to the table. 'Gracie, make some more tea, and Phylly, fetch those fresh scones out of the pantry, please.'

Phylly's legs felt as if they were filled with jelly as she made her way to the pantry where she stood quietly for a few moments breathing slowly to try and calm her racing heart down. She couldn't quite believe that Edwin was here, that he'd come back, but he was definitely here, she could hear his voice with its lovely American twang as he answered a barrage of questions. She swallowed hard to stop herself from crying – she mustn't make a fool of herself because a treacherous thought had crept into her mind. Edwin might have come back, but did he still want her to be his girl? After all he'd been through he might have changed his mind and wanted to get back to America as soon as he could.

Carrying the scones through to the kitchen, Phylly

was almost knocked off her feet by a whirlwind in striped pyjamas rushing past her.

'Edwin!' Jimmy launched himself at Edwin, who stood up and caught the boy in his arms. 'You've come home. I knew you would. I've been to Thanksgiving today and it was as good as you said it was. I even liked the cranberry sauce.'

Edwin laughed and ruffled Jimmy's hair. 'I'm real glad you got to celebrate Thanksgiving, Jimmy.'

'What happened to you?' Gracie asked when they were all once again sitting around the kitchen table with cups of tea in front of them and Edwin had satisfied Florrie by eating two scones with butter and jam.

'Our plane was in trouble – two engines were gone and we were losing height. Captain ordered us to bail out and he stayed on to try and bring her home to England. He did it, too, just got her over the Channel and landed at an RAF base. Those of us who bailed out had to do our best to make it on our own behind enemy lines.'

Phylly was relieved to be sitting down as the truth behind Edwin's disappearance came pouring out.

'Have you all come back?' Jacob asked.

Edwin shook his head. 'I'm the only who made it home. There was a strong crosswind and we were blown far apart from each other. The rest were captured and are now POWs but I was lucky and got picked up by the Resistance. They hid me, kept moving me from place to place until I was passed over to the Allied side again. It took a long time to find my way home.'

'Does your mother know you're safe?' Bea asked.

'She sure does. A telegram's been sent and I've written to her.'

'She'll be so relieved,' Ned said.

Phylly knew how worried Ned had been about Edwin's mother. 'Why don't you write to her, Ned? I'm sure she'd be glad to hear from you.'

Edwin nodded. 'She sure would.'

Ned looked unsure.

'Mom talked about you very fondly. Go on, write to her.'

'I will then, thank you.' Ned caught Phylly's eye and smiled warmly at her.

Perhaps he'll get to meet Edwin's mother again, Phylly thought, and have another chance to tell her how he felt.

'So, what's been happening here while I've been gone?' Edwin asked.

'Aunt Min died,' Jimmy said abruptly. 'She left a letter asking Bea to be my new mum and she's going to adopt me.'

Edwin listened as Bea and Jimmy told him what had happened. 'I'm real sorry to hear that, Jimmy, but I know Bea will look after you real good, be just like a proper mom to you.'

'Come on, Jimmy, it's time you went to bed,' Bea said. 'You'll be able to see Edwin again soon.'

'You sure will. I'm done with missions, that was my last one.'

'You'll be going home, then?' Ned asked.

Edwin shook his head. 'No, sir. I've volunteered to become a paddlefoot.'

He wasn't going back to America, Phylly thought. Was there a chance for them after all?

'What's that?' Gracie asked.

'It's what flyboys call ground staff and it's what I'm going to do now.' Edwin glanced at his watch. 'I'm sorry but I'm gonna have to go – they weren't keen on me coming out on my first night back, but I just had to come and see you folks. I promise I'll be back soon.' He stood up. 'Phylly, would you mind showing me out?'

'Of course.' She followed him to the door.

'See you soon, everybody,' Edwin said. 'It sure is good to be back.'

As soon as they were outside with the door closed behind them, Edwin grabbed hold of both of her hands.

'Oh Phylly, I've missed you so much . . . ' Edwin's voice cracked.

'And I've missed you and I'm so sorry I said I was too scared to be your girl when you asked me at the dance . . . when I heard your plane had gone down I regretted it . . . I wished I had said yes and grabbed the chance while we had it. I kept hoping and hoping you'd come back.'

He looked at her, studying her face as if he were

drinking it all in. 'I thought about you all the time I was away. I wanted to get back to you so we could be together, it was the thought of it kept me going, made me determined to see you again.'

'If you'd still like me to, I'll be your girl,' Phylly said.

Edwin smiled and stepped closer. 'Really?'

She nodded. 'I was worried you might have changed your mind about me.'

'Never. I'm so glad you changed yours . . . Phylly, will you be my girl – will you marry me, please?'

Phylly stared at him, taken aback by what he'd asked her. 'Marry you?'

'Why not? Why wait? We waited before and I wish we hadn't.'

'Me, too.' She smiled.

'So, will you?'

Phylly laughed and threw her arms around him, hugging him tight, not ever wanting to let him go. She'd turned down a chance to be with Edwin before and she wasn't going to make the same mistake twice.

'Yes, please.'

Acknowledgements

A Home from Home first came out in ebook back in 2018 and I always hoped that one day it would be published in paperback too. This story is one that is close to my heart, being set on my home turf in Norfolk, and with a good dollop of family history inspiring the story. A huge thank you to my fantastic editor, Rebecca Roy, and the team at Sphere for making this wish come true!

With all historical books, researching the facts is helped by others. Thank you to my parents who answered countless questions about wartime Norfolk. The archives of the Imperial War Museum provided me with invaluable first-hand accounts of Land Girls, and Norfolk Library service many research books.

A big thank you to all the readers and bloggers who read and review my books, and keep in touch.

My dear writing friends in the Strictly Saga group and Norfolk & Suffolk RNA group are a fabulous bunch and I am so fortunate to have you in my life – thank you all.

Lastly, thank you to David for his incredible support.

Dear Reader,

I hope you enjoyed reading *A Home from Home* as much as I loved writing it. The story was first published as an eight-part serial in *The People's Friend* – where I started my writing career submitting and selling short stories to the magazine. It was an ambition of mine to write a serial for them, and with *A Home from Home* I finally managed it.

I've always loved this story as it combines so many aspects of the Second World War that are fascinating and have great storytelling potential, as well as family history from that time.

My mum lived at the real Catchetts Farm during the war and having always loved that name, I wanted to use it for the story. I wear a ring from Catchetts Farm which my grandmother gave me. When she found it at the side of the range at the farm, it was broken and had the stone missing from the setting, so I had it mended and a sapphire put in and have worn it ever since.

Other aspects of the story are based on true events such as my dad having to hide from enemy aircraft shooting at civilians while out on his bicycle, and Land Girls capturing who they thought was a spy with their pitchforks, holding him prisoner until the police arrived.

I love to hear from readers – it is one of the greatest joys of being a writer – so do please get in touch. You can contact me via my website www.rosiehendry.com or via my Facebook page Rosie Hendry Books, Twitter @hendry_rosie or follow me on Instagram rosiehendryauthor. Subscribing to my newsletter is the best way to keep up with all my latest book news – you can do this on my website.

If you have time and would like to share your thoughts about this book, do please leave a star rating or review. I appreciate each one and it's wonderful to hear what you think of the story. It helps me with my writing knowing what readers like and encourages new readers to try my books. Thank you!

With my warmest wishes,

Rosie

Read on for the heart-warming beginning to *The Mother's Day Club* by Rosie Hendry – an uplifting family saga that celebrates friendship in wartime Britain

Chapter 1

East End, London – 3 September 1939

It was a beautiful late-summer day with a blue sky soaring high above the East End streets and Marianne Archer was in a hurry, her gas mask box banging against her hip and her heavy suitcase making her slower than usual. Her step faltered as she spotted a newspaper billboard set out on the pavement ahead of her and read the bold message printed in stark black and white: 'Peace or War?' It made her catch her breath. Would it *really* come to war?

She'd listened to the wireless, read the newspapers and seen all the preparations going on around London, and she knew full well that the country was teetering on the brink of war, but deep down she'd held on to the hope that somehow, by some miracle, it wouldn't come to it, and that something would happen even now, at the last minute, to stop it.

Looking up at the sky, which looked so perfect today, without a single cloud to mar the blue, you'd never know what was going on, she thought, never know what chaos was probably about to be unleashed.

Pushing on past the billboard, she followed the stream of people heading to the local school where all evacuees had been instructed to gather. The sight of so many evacuees carrying their luggage through the streets had become a familiar one in the last few days. The children had been the first to go; now it was the turn of the expectant mothers, and Marianne was glad to be leaving, not just because of the threat of war and what it might bring here, but because London had turned sour for her. What had started out as an exciting adventure and blossoming career had gone badly wrong and she was eager for a new start.

Inside the school, she joined the end of the queue of people waiting to register their arrival, relieved to put down her suitcase at last. Looking around her, she saw that the hall was already busy – not just the expectant mothers and young children who were preparing to leave, but also their relatives and even some husbands too, who'd clearly come to see them off. The noise level was rising steadily among the swirl of cigarette smoke, people having to speak ever louder to make themselves heard above the din of chatter, grizzling children and even a few weeping women.

The queue shuffled forwards slowly. The woman ahead of Marianne had to heave her fractious toddler up on to her hip, her swollen stomach making it impossible for her to hold the child in her arms in front of her. Nudging her brown suitcase forward with her foot, Marianne looked down at her own growing belly – it was impossible now to do up more than the top three buttons on her thin summer coat; there was no hiding the fact that she was expecting any more.

'Next.' The mother in front of Marianne had been dealt with and moved off, heaving her toddler and string bag of belongings with her. The WVS woman sitting at the desk looked up at Marianne through her round glasses and smiled. 'Your name?'

'Marianne Archer.'

She ran her finger down the list, found Marianne's name and put a tick beside it. 'If you'd like to take a seat . . . ' She looked around the hall and shrugged: there wasn't an empty seat to be had. 'We weren't expecting *quite* so many family members to turn up. We'll be leaving shortly anyway, so you won't have long to wait.'

'All right, thank you.' Marianne picked up her suitcase and went to stand by the open door where the fresh air, or at least what passed for that around here, was blowing in on a welcome breeze, ruffling her dark brown, shoulder-length wavy hair. She could smell the distinctive tang of the East End – chimney smoke from the many homes and factories combined with a salty twist from the docks and the River Thames. Proper fresh, clean air that didn't irritate your nose was something she was looking forward to again, along with wide skies, space and greenery. She had lived in London for the past four years, coming to work here when she was sixteen, but the city had never truly felt like home. In fact, Marianne dearly missed the countryside, so now, being evacuated to a place that didn't have a shop on every corner, buses one after the other, or street after street of terraced houses, would be no hardship for her.

They set off walking through the streets towards Liverpool Street station a short while later, forming a raggle-taggle line behind a WVS evacuation officer in her smart green uniform, who, like a modern-day Pied Piper, was leading them to safety. Many of the evacuees carried luggage that looked inadequate for the journey ahead, their belongings stuffed into string or paper bags, sacks or cardboard boxes; not many of the expectant mothers had a suitcase like Marianne.

As they passed through the streets where some of them lived, the evacuees' neighbours stood in their front doorways watching them go and calling out tearful farewells.

'Look after yourself, ducks.'

'We'll keep the 'ome fires burning for yer.'

There was a real sense of loss in the air as part of their community was leaving, Marianne thought, looking at the women who were waving them off and wiping their eyes with their spotlessly clean handkerchiefs. The East Enders were a close-knit bunch, sharing their ups and downs, helping each other out, so to have mothers evacuated was like taking the beating heart out of their homes, and they'd be sorely missed by those they left behind.

She couldn't say the same about herself, though. Her departure was leaving nothing but an empty room behind, and her landlady probably had a new tenant lined up already. There was no one around here to be sad that she was going, but that was the way she'd wanted it. Moving to the East End to work in a clothing factory two months ago and live anonymously had been the best thing to do, but seeing the emotion and heartfelt tears of friends and family saying their goodbyes tugged at her heart and prodded at the loneliness she'd felt since then. Making the best of a situation wasn't always easy, her gran had often said, but that's what she'd had to do.

'Dad says to tell you, Chamberlain says it's war!' A boy hurtled out of one of the houses, broadcasting the news as he ran up to one mother just ahead of Marianne, grabbing at her hand. 'He just said so on the wireless.'

Surprisingly, no one stopped at the momentous news, the formation kept on moving, and although it wasn't unexpected, the certainty that they were now at war with Germany made Marianne's heart sink. It was little more than twenty years since the last time they'd been pitched against this enemy, and she'd grown up with the shadow of the last war blighting her life – her father had been killed in the last few months before she was born. She'd heard the stories of the muddy trenches and the huge death toll, seen the men with shattered lives and missing limbs. That had been the war to end all wars, and yet here it was, happening all over again.

The sudden sound of an air-raid siren began to wail out across the rooftops, its eerie cry rising and falling again and again, like some wounded animal. It changed the mood like the flick of a switch, and the formation faltered. People halted, looking up at the sky, their eyes wide in shock. Several mothers began to cry, and toddlers, picking up on the women's distress, added their own wails.

Marianne looked around her, uncertain what to do. Could the Germans be about to bomb them so soon? A passing red double-decker bus pulled over to the side of the road, the driver and passengers spilling out in panic and quickly disappearing down side streets. Should they do the same?

One of the evacuation officers clapped her hands and shouted, 'Keep moving!'

'Don't stop! We need to get to Liverpool Street,' another added, working her way down the column encouraging everyone to move off again. They did as they were told; no one questioned it or ran off, but they quickened their pace, adults picking up any toddlers who were too slow, everyone anxious to reach the station and get under cover.

'You'd best go back, Granddad,' a young woman near Marianne said to the old man who was accompanying her. 'If they comes, you can't run. I can't let the Nazis catch you.'

'Curse 'em. I ain't letting you go alone.' The old man shook his stick at the sky and kept on walking, doing his best to keep up.

There'd been no sound of aeroplanes approaching or bombs falling, but Marianne still felt hugely relieved when they finally arrived and had the domed roof of Liverpool Street station, with its ornate iron beams, between her and any enemy planes.

'This way,' the leading evacuation officer shouted in her loud plummy voice. She led them across the busy station concourse where the air smelt of burning coal from the steam engines, parting the people hurrying to and fro, like Moses had the Red Sea.

As they reached the barrier at platform ten, the steady sound of the all-clear rang out and the atmosphere lightened. They were safe – for now, at least.

'Evacuees only on the platform,' another WVS woman called. 'There isn't room for everyone so you'll need to say your goodbyes here.'

Marianne side-stepped the families saying their tearful farewells, grateful now that she didn't have the emotional wrench of having to leave loved ones behind. Quite the opposite, in fact: she was glad to be going. From the way some of the expectant mothers were clinging to their husbands or relatives, tears streaming down their faces, they didn't share her feelings.

Walking past the railway guards who stood by the barrier to make sure that no other family members sneaked on to the platform, she headed to the far end of the train that stood ready to take them to safety and climbed aboard a carriage. She chose a compartment, slid open the door, stowed her case and settled herself by the window facing the engine, so she'd be able to enjoy the view as they travelled.

As Marianne waited for the train to fill up, her mind wandered over the possibilities of what lay ahead. She tried to calm the tingle of apprehension that had lodged itself in her chest, visualising what it might be like, who she would be billeted with. She hoped it was someone nice; she'd done her best to look presentable, wearing the new dress she'd designed and made herself with its pin-tuck detail on the bodice, in a beautiful deep green fabric that went well with her green eyes. It was important to make a good first impression – another of her gran's many sayings. She smiled as she pictured her saying it so many times as she'd grown up, though what she would say about the situation Marianne had got herself into she hardly dared think. Perhaps it was just as well that Gran had passed away a year ago now, because she'd have been bitterly disappointed in her, and that would have been nearly as hard to bear as her own anger at her stupidity and naivety.

'Excuse me, is that seat taken?'

Marianne was pulled out of her thoughts and looked up to see an auburn-haired young woman standing in the open doorway of the compartment and pointing at the empty seat opposite her. In fact, it was the only empty seat left – while Marianne had been absorbed in her own world, the other seats had filled up with another expectant mother and her two little girls and two other women who had pulled out their knitting and were already busy, their needles clicking.

She smiled at her. 'No.'

'Oh, thank Gawd.' She shuffled past the other occupants' legs and stuffed her bag of belongings in the overhead luggage rack then plopped herself down on the seat. 'I'd begun to think I'd 'ave to stand all the way to wherever we're goin'. The train's filled up so fast, but I 'ad to stay with my Arthur for as long as I could, and then the WVS woman was chivvyin' me to get a shift on or the train would go without me.' She paused for breath and stuck out her hand with a friendly smile. 'I'm Sally Parker.'

Marianne shook her hand. 'Marianne Archer.' She smiled at the other woman, noticing her red-rimmed eyes and pink-tipped nose.

'Pleased to meet you, Marianne. Are you looking forward to this? Cos I ain't, but my Arthur said I 'ad to go for the sake of this one.' She stroked her stomach, which protruded from her slender frame like a football, pushing out the front of her floral dress. 'He's going to enlist for the Army right away, not wait to be called up, so he won't be around here anyway. Did your hubby want you to go too?'

Marianne nodded.

'He come and see you off?'

'No.'

'That's a shame.' Sally frowned. 'Couldn't he get time off work?'

'He's in the Navy, at sea.' The words tripped awkwardly off Marianne's tongue.

'Well, he'll be glad you're on your way to safety.'

Marianne nodded, relieved when they were distracted by a sudden loud blast from the guard's whistle outside. Soon the carriage began to move, the platform slipping past, as the steam engine at the head of the train belched out great chuffs of sooty smoke that swirled up to the ornate station roof.

'Where do yer think we're going?' Sally asked as they cleared the gloom of the station and slipped out into the beautiful sunshine.

Marianne looked at this young woman, who suddenly seemed very vulnerable and nervous in spite of all her chatter. 'I don't know, we haven't been told, but as we're leaving from Liverpool Street, I'd guess it must be somewhere in the east, not Devon or Wales.'

'Right out in the countryside, then?'

'Yes. And away from where they might drop bombs.'

Sally stared out of the window for a few moments. 'I ain't been out to the countryside much before, I've been 'op picking a couple of times down in Kent, but that's all.'

'It will be different from London, but I'm sure it'll be fine,' Marianne said. 'Better to be safe.'

Sally nodded, leaning against the back of her seat. 'That's what my Arthur said.' She rubbed her hand across her stomach. 'So, when's yours due? Mine should be 'ere by Christmas.'

'Late January for me.'

'Will your husband be home before then to see yer?' Sally asked. 'Arthur's promised to come and visit me when 'e can, though once he's in the Army it'll be up to them when he's allowed.'

'I'm not sure.' Marianne looked down at the still-shiny gold ring on the third finger of her left hand. She'd bought it herself.

'Well, yer can always write letters in the meantime, can't yer?' Sally said as they passed row upon row of tightly packed terrace houses.

'Of course.'

'My Arthur says he can't wait to get my first letter . . . '

Marianne listened to Sally chattering on, the young

woman having enough to say for both of them, while the wheels of the train clickety-clacked beneath them. Through the window the streets gradually gave way to more greenery, space and light, and the sight made her heart lift. Wherever they were heading had to be better for her than London had turned out to be.

Chapter 2

Rookery House, Great Plumstead, Norfolk

Thea Thornton flicked her wrists, sending the clean white sheet billowing out to settle over the mattress of the single bed, and breathed in the smell of the lavender that she'd picked and dried this summer to scent the linen press. Tucking in the sides and corners, she worked quickly, adding another sheet on top, then a blanket, turning back the top end of the upper sheet over the thicker woollen cloth to make a neat finish, and finally spreading out the dusky-pink feather eiderdown over the top. Pulling the eiderdown straight and smoothing the satiny material with her hand, she smiled at the thought of who'd be sleeping in here tonight: their evacuee – a child who'd been whisked away from London because of the risk of war.

She was looking forward to a child living here with her at Rookery House, having the chance to give them a home away from home, one where they'd feel safe and be well looked after. It was both exciting and terrifying in equal measure. It would be a massive change in her life and for the evacuee too, who would not only have been forced to leave their family to come and live with strangers, but would be moving to the alien environment of the countryside. Life in Great Plumstead was a world away from the busy streets of London, and Thea knew from experience that such a change would take some adjusting to.

She'd made the move herself, although in reverse – from here to London; but she'd been an adult when she'd taken the plunge and already had some experience of living somewhere different as she'd gone to drive ambulances in France during the Great War. Still, going from village life to the city had been a huge shock; the noise and busyness had been overwhelming at first. She'd longed to be able to see further than the end of the road. The world seemed to have shrunk, closed in by the buildings that were packed in so close together that the views of the sky were limited to patches above the crowded streets. It had taken her a long time to adjust. Starting her business and growing it had absorbed her time and energy but it had eventually led her back here now, some seventeen years later, after she'd sold up and returned home just three months ago to buy this house. Now, with the country teetering on the verge of war, it was probably none too soon either.

Thea looked around the room, with its cast-iron fireplace, sash window overlooking the back garden, wooden wardrobe and chest of drawers that shone with elbow grease and beeswax polish. She still pinched herself sometimes, hardly believing that she was actually living here, the owner of Rookery House, the house that she'd loved from as long ago as she could remember. As a child she had often stopped to admire the house, saying to herself that one day, if she could, she'd live here, and now . . . here she was, forty-one years old and with her life-long dream come true.

Rookery House was a detached Victorian house, set back from the road, lying a quarter of a mile out of the village with a generous three and a half acres of land to go with it, which looked out over woods and fields. Its name came from the rookery in the stand of tall elm trees some fifty yards down the lane from the house, where the birds filled the air with their plaintive cawing in the spring, while they tended their chicks in their twiggy nests. Thea loved them, the sound of their calls instantly calming her, and their flying antics on a windy day making her smile, their sheer joy in riding the wind plain to see.

This house, with its five bedrooms, was far bigger than she needed just for herself, but Thea was intent on filling it up. She'd invited her friend Hettie to come and live with her, the older woman having recently retired from her job as cook up at Great Plumstead Hall. Reuben, Thea's older brother, had accepted her invitation too, although he refused to live in the house, preferring to set up home in an old railway carriage he'd bought and sited over by the orchard. He said he wanted peace and quiet, and it was probably a wise move with the way Hettie liked to talk, but he often joined them for meals. The loss of his wife the previous year had hit him hard, so a move to live nearby had been a compromise, one that suited them both: she could keep an eye on him, but he could go his own way without bothering anyone.

So for the five bedrooms, this one would soon be the evacuee's, she and Hettie had one each, and the other two would be ready for anyone who needed them. Thea liked having people around her and whoever might come to stay in those rooms in the future would be most welcome.

Going over to the window, she looked out over the back garden to where Reuben and her sister's two boys – her nephews, Jack and Edwin – were digging a hole for the Anderson shelter. It looked like it must surely be big enough soon, the pile of earth they'd dug out like a monstrous mole hill on the grass. Was it really necessary to have it? she wondered. Well, it was best to be prepared, and with the way things were heading most people were saying it was only a matter of *when*, not *if*, war would be declared; but ever the optimist, Thea refused to give up hope that peace would prevail and she'd hold on to that until proved wrong.